INTO THE MAELSTROM

TALES OF THE FEISTY DRUID™ BOOK 7

CANDY CRUM

MICHAEL ANDERLE

Larry Omans
Micky Cocker

If we missed anyone, please let us know!

Editor
Jen McDonnell

INTO THE MAELSTROM

CHAPTER ONE

Ten Days Earlier

Over the past couple of days, Arryn had readied her things and centered herself for the trip that was to come. They were traveling to a whole new land, and she found herself a little nervous.

On top of that, she had to ready Corrine as well. She was overly excited and not really thinking much of the dangers. Then again, as Arryn was the adult, that was more her job, anyway. She decided to let Corrine have her fun and make the girl's preparations for her.

Leaving the Dark Forest was always bittersweet for her. Every time, she felt a stab of pain and worry, even while her belly was riddled with excitement. Today, however, would be much different.

In the last several months, the Dark Forest had experienced a lot of unnatural funerals, the deaths all having been caused by war. Today would be the first true druid funeral since Arryn had first come to the Dark Forest.

For many—well, for most—funerals were considered a sad

occasion. They were less a celebration of life and more a mourning of loss. For the druids, when someone passed naturally, it was truly a beautiful thing.

Ushering an Elder from this life into the next was considered a great honor, because it didn't happen often. While druids were not immortal by any means, they certainly outlived any other human.

At one hundred and seventeen years old, the Elder Lida would pass from this life into the next; she had been very old when she had come to the Dark Forest, but her magic allowed her to live decades longer than what was expected.

As part of the Chieftain's immediate family, Arryn was invited to be part of the process of her moving on. Arryn looked over the crowd and saw Celine and her father in attendance. That warmed her heart.

Arryn held Lida's left hand, and Elysia held her right as they walked with her one last time to the *Heilig* tree. This tree was the largest in the forest—hundreds of feet tall, and thicker than Cathillian was tall. Its colossal size was because whenever an Elder passed, they expended the rest of their energy into its roots.

With a smile on her face, Lida turned and waved to everyone. Since the battle, she had grown increasingly weak and knew it was her time. She decided to take to the tree with her family, before death claimed her in her sleep and deprived her of the honor.

"I traveled here in the very beginning, with our Chieftain Alexander as my guide. I trained with the Founder himself, along with Alexander, who only seemed like a young boy back then." She laughed. "He is *still* a boy to me, but he has grown strong and fearless. Never once did he lead us wrong. It was an honor to live alongside him and his family, who would become my family, in this very forest."

She smiled as she extended her hands out to her sides. "I am honored beyond words to have my family here with me to experience this. To feed the tree is to feed the forest, to provide weapons and armor to those who pass the *Versuch* and go on to protect this forest. Today, I become part of the tree."

She looked to Arryn, who held the staff that Elysia had crafted from the *Heilig*. Arryn smiled in return.

Lida took several deep breaths as she began to waver a bit. It was taking all the energy she had left to stand at that point.

She looked at Arryn, then to Elysia, the smile never leaving her face. She gave a curt nod. "It's time."

Arryn had only seen this twice, and both times had been before she was fully acclimated. She would have to rely on Elysia and learn what to do from her movements.

Elysia stepped forward, once again grabbing hold of the woman's hand, and Arryn followed suit on the opposite side. They helped her sit on the ground, then assisted her in leaning back against the tree.

Clutching the woman's hand tight in her own, Elysia smiled, leaned forward, and placed a kiss on the Elder's knuckles before laying her hand back in her lap. Elysia nodded at Arryn, and she did the same before placing the hand she held on top of the other. The old woman smiled at Elysia before turning to Arryn.

"You have come a long way, child. You are a champion of our people. One day, hopefully many, many decades from now, you will be here where I am, and you will have this honor. You have already. Live your life to the fullest. Have lots of babies. Have lots of incredible battles. Never stop living."

Arryn was moved by the woman's words. She didn't know about the baby part—that wasn't something she cared to think about for several years to come—but she certainly planned to spend her foreseeable future righting wrongs that had been made in the world.

Elysia stood and backed away, and Arryn did the same.

Lida's eyes flashed green, and the old *Heilig* began to creak and crack as the branches began to grow. Arryn could see the place in the tree where Elysia had taken a branch for her bow and staff. Though Elysia had somewhat healed the spot, Lida's magic was helping it grow back even thicker than it had been before.

Arryn's eyes flashed black as she rolled her right wrist, a ball of light appearing in her hand. She tossed it into the air, and the ball split into several more beautiful, dancing lights and hovered over Lida.

The old woman's eyes widened as she smiled, a tear sliding down her cheek. She looked to Arryn and mouthed the words, 'thank you,' before looking back to the lights.

More orbs came to join those, and Arryn turned her head to see that Celine and her father had thrown them from their place in the crowd of druids who came to witness this bittersweet tradition. The white and yellow orbs twinkled overhead, shining down on Lida as the sun tried to peek through the thick canopy above.

Soon, Arryn began to feel the life energy dwindling, and Elysia once again approached the fading Elder. Arryn did the same, coming to rest on her other side.

"Now, we aid her in her journey," Elysia said.

Arryn had already been told what that meant, so she knew what to expect.

Elysia reached out, placing one of her hands over Lida's and the other over the woman's heart. Arryn reached forward and placed her hands a few inches away from Elysia's, careful not to touch her.

Together, as practiced, Elysia and Arryn said, "Thank you for everything you have given us in this life. May your next be full of love and light."

Lida closed her eyes as she continued to push her magic to the tree. Arryn's and Elysia's eyes flashed green before they closed them and lowered their heads. Each of them began to use their magic to ease the Elder's passing, painlessly draining the life that was left, ensuring she did not suffer or linger unnecessarily.

As Lida took her final breath, Arryn and Elysia lifted their hands and opened their eyes. Everyone then knelt to the ground, silence filling the air for several moments as they showed their respect for the woman who had passed.

When Arryn and Elysia finally stood, they backed away to make room for the several warriors who came to retrieve Lida's body. Arryn already remembered what came next, but Elysia reminded her anyway. What remained of Lida would be placed on a pyre, and her ashes would be spread around the base of the *Heilig*, allowing her to truly become part of the tree.

Now that she was older and had more understanding of the world and life and what it meant to die, Arryn hoped she would one day receive the honor of being made part of the beautiful *Heilig*.

But that certainly wouldn't be anytime soon.

"I'm glad we waited to leave," Arryn said. "I would have been devastated to have missed that."

"That was pretty amazing, what you did," Elysia said as she escorted her away. "Those lights were beautiful, and it obviously made her feel special. That was a very nice touch."

Arryn smiled and shrugged. "She was an important part of the village, and she deserved something special. We all do when we go."

"I couldn't agree more." Elysia sighed as she continued to walk with Arryn. "I suppose you will all be leaving now, right?"

Nodding, Arryn said, "Yes. We don't know the condition of Bast and Cleo's homeland, and the problem with the bandits needs to be dealt with now rather than later. Otherwise, you might have another war on your hands, and it's obvious they had some pretty nasty weapons. It's better to catch them off guard while we have the chance, and get to Kemet as soon as possible to fight off whatever monsters have been plaguing the area."

"I know and understand the reasons, but it doesn't make it any easier. You guys are everything to me—Corrine, too. You'll be almost a week away, and after you leave there, it'll be more than two weeks' distance. If there's trouble, there's no way for me to get to you fast enough."

Cathillian wandered up and wrapped his arms around his mother's shoulders. "Aw, don't worry, Mom. Arryn has me to protect her, so obviously, everything will be just fine."

Elysia laughed. "As strong as you are, son, I think you might have that backwards."

He shook his head. "Damn. *Never* any respect around here."

Elysia, Celine, and Christopher all accompanied them as they finished readying their things. Arryn was worried about her father staying behind, but she knew it was the right decision.

She had no idea how it would affect him to go directly back into battle, and she didn't want to hinder his progress. He was also doing very well with his training, but she wanted to see him improve even more before getting in another fight.

"Make sure you come back to me," Christopher said, his hands on either side of his daughter's face. "We have so much catching up to do, so much more we can learn from one another."

Arryn smiled as her hands came to rest on his. "Trust me. I'll be back. Can't get rid of me that easily."

Cathillian snorted and opened his mouth to speak, but Arryn was quick to interrupt. "Yeah, yeah, Cat; you've tried to get rid of me and failed. You need new jokes."

He looked at her with a slightly shocked expression. "Now, why would you think I would say something like that? See, you're always interrupting me. You didn't even give me a chance to say what I was really gonna say."

Arryn looked at him with an amused expression, putting all her weight onto one foot as she relaxed into a condescending pose, her arms crossed over her chest. "Yeah? Please, do tell us. What were you going to say instead?"

He stood there for a moment, his eyes locked on hers, before he finally said, "I was just going to say, why would anyone want to be without you? You're just the *bestest*."

Arryn hesitated for a moment, a smile spreading across her face. "You're a damn dirty liar."

Cathillian nodded. "Yeah... That *did* kind of hurt a little to say."

"Mmhmm. I thought it might have," Arryn said, rolling her eyes. "One more crack out of you, and I'm leaving you here."

Elysia smiled and stepped forward, grabbing hold of them and pulling them tight to her. "I'm gonna miss both of you."

CHAPTER TWO

Esmerelda stepped out of the sea, naked as the day she came into this world. Though the news of her husband's death had reached her, a subtle smile spread across her lips as she prepared herself for what would come next.

For years, she had been forced to watch from the sidelines, never having a say in anything her husband—or any other man, for that matter—did or said. They were able to do anything they liked, take anything they liked—including women—and nothing could be said or done about it.

That was about to change.

Locke had been their leader, a king among degenerates and lowlifes. Though it wasn't the life she had envisioned for herself, at the very least, she should have been seen as his queen. She should have been just as important as he was, and respected as such. Instead, she and the other women were seen as little more than slaves.

Locke had worked for Adrien for too long. Adrien treated anyone who worked for him like trash, servants who weren't worth his time. All the long-dead Chancellor had respected was power. If someone had it, he was either afraid of it and would end the threat immediately, or he would employ them, if he believed they were controllable.

Locke had learned many of those same qualities—but even the tyrant Adrien had women working for him. Locke, however, saw women as weaknesses; they had no place by his side. Not even his own wife.

He deserved to die, she thought to herself. *Now is* our *time.*

Along the Farriage Coast, they didn't have stick-built buildings. Instead, they built sturdy tents that could withstand the winds coming off the sea; portable housing in case they ever needed to disappear at a moment's notice.

In the center was the largest tent, the one that had been built specifically for Locke's meetings. It could hold two hundred men and still leave standing room for the slave girls to make their way through with drinks.

Enough room for them to be accosted as they walked past. She growled to herself as the tent came into view.

A young woman stepped out to meet her, not saying a word as she held out a robe. Still naked, Esmerelda took the robe and loosely wrapped it around herself, tying it, though she didn't really care if it were open or closed.

"Is everything in place?" Esmerelda asked.

She saw the curt nod out of her peripheral. "Yes. A meeting was called, just as you suspected. Johnson made it back from the battle alive, but he suffered many injuries. He has pulled the men together to tell them that Locke was killed."

Esmerelda almost laughed. "They'll no doubt have some form of election, or brawl to decide the next leader."

She could see a smile pull at the corner of the girl's mouth. "They won't have the opportunity."

Indeed, they won't, Esmerelda thought to herself. They walked the rest of the way in silence, each lost in her own thoughts.

The tent was at capacity, and the flaps were pulled open, so the rest of the men could gather around outside and hear the announcements.

That made Esmerelda very happy. It would make what she had to do much easier. Chin held high, she made her way to the front of the tent.

She gave a brief pause as she looked at the chair that was reserved for her—her "throne" that was not a throne at all. It had been put together with little care; its edges hadn't even been smoothed down, so it gave her splinters at times. She almost growled at the chair that had once been designated for her as she passed it.

Even the two hundred or so chairs in the audience had been put together with more effort. Her husband's chair was everything one would imagine a vigilante throne to be. The back of it was as tall as any man standing next to it, and the seat was wide enough to accommodate Locke and no less than two women, which were often present, even in front of Esmerelda.

It was a physical reminder of exactly how important he was, and how *un*important she, and every other woman around, were.

Johnson was already standing at the front of the tent, not daring to sit in Locke's vacated seat, out of respect—but she wasn't prepared to do any such thing.

Completely ignoring the spot that was once hers, she sauntered across the space with nothing shy of a confident gait before sitting in the throne, crossing her legs, and laying her hands on the armrests of the chair—though she had to reach a little.

There were several gasps, and then whispers as the men pointed and talked amongst themselves. Their brows furrowed angrily.

"You shouldn't be here," Johnson said quietly to Esmerelda.

She gave a bright smile, cocking her head to the side. "Actually, I believe it's *you* who shouldn't be up here. As much of a rotten bastard as he was, Locke is dead, and I am his widow."

Johnson laughed, and several other men in the audience

followed suit. Esmerelda only smiled as she watched them, willing them to keep their attention on her.

As they savored their laughter and the joke that a woman would dare do such a thing in their midst, the slave girls were weaving through the aisles with mugs of ale in one hand, and their other hand free.

"I'm afraid you are greatly mistaken. No *woman* will replace any man here—especially a man like Locke. You'd be wise to get your ass off that throne." Johnson was quite a bit more serious now, turning his body so he was fully facing her. The men in the audience began to reflect his shift in tone.

From somewhere in the crowd, she heard a familiar shriek and knew one of the men had grabbed a woman. It happened every assembly, but this would certainly be the last time.

Reaching down, but making sure not to break eye contact, Esmerelda put her hand in the pocket of her robe. Tucked inside, as requested, was a knife. With a flick of her thumb, she freed it from its sheath and pulled it from her pocket.

Loosely holding onto the blade, she allowed the hilt to fall forward before flicking it back against her wrist, repeating the process several times as she smiled at the man standing before her.

"Oh, Johnson. The winds of change are blowing and have been for a *very* long time—apparently you haven't noticed. You can sit down now." She waved him off with her free hand, then turned her eyes away from him, coldly dismissing him.

Without saying a word, Johnson balled up his fists and took two very heavy steps toward her.

A knife to his abdomen stopped him cold.

His eyes widened as he stared at her across the ten feet that separated them. She continued with her wicked smile, waving the now empty hand that once held the knife. She stood and slowly walked over then wrapped her hand around the hilt.

"You see, a woman *will* take Locke's place. *I* am that woman.

Unfortunately, you won't get the chance to see just how great we become," she said, twisting the blade and pulling it free.

Johnson's hands struggled to cover the gaping wound in his stomach as he fell to his knees. Esmerelda looked out at the crowd. Her free hand was lightning fast as she gripped a handful of the man's long, blonde hair. She yanked his head back and stabbed the blade through his throat.

Then she pulled her knife free at an angle, opening the wound further. Blood sprayed everywhere, and she used his hair as leverage to toss him to the floor.

Every man in the audience stared on with wide eyes, obviously enraged. There were several cries of anger, and they moved to surge forward, but the slaves were too fast.

Every woman threw their knees or elbows into the guts or groins of the men they were standing next to before pulling hidden blades from what little clothing they were allowed to wear. Those knives immediately went to throats, holding steady as Esmerelda stood at the front with her glowing smile.

"On your knees, gentlemen," Esmerelda said. "I'd hate for anything to happen to you, just when we have the opportunity to start such a *beautiful* friendship."

There were only a few moments of hesitation before the men began dropping to their knees.

The women widened their stances as they stood behind their targets, hands wrapped around hair with firm grips, while knives were placed firmly against carotid arteries.

"You see, not only was my husband killed, but many of your friends were, as well. That leaves you slightly outnumbered. We have seen this coming for a *long* time; we have been preparing for such a wondrous day. Today, we reclaim our freedom. Today, we show you *exactly* the same courtesy you have always shown to us."

Several of the men tried to argue, no doubt lashing out with wounded pride, but Esmerelda and her warrior goddesses were quick to stop it. With a wave of Esmerelda's hand, the knives pressed harder, many drawing blood.

"You *will* fight for me. You *will* win. You will do *anything* and *every*thing that I tell you, and you will do so without fail. Because if you *do* fail me, I can promise the punishment for that treachery will be far worse than anything Locke could ever think of.

"During our many years in Arcadia and our time out here, being unable to speak, beaten down if we dared to have an opinion, we've spent a lot of time locked in our heads, plotting exactly what to do when the time came."

She paused as she watched the fight fall away from the men's faces. One by one, they were accepting what was happening—the shift of power, and exactly what it could mean if they didn't go along with it.

Esmerelda extended her hands out to her sides as she spoke again. "I will say this once, and you will obey and respect what I tell you, or you will die where you kneel. We have been degraded for the last time. We have been slapped, beaten, and raped for the last time. We have been lied to, cheated on, fucked over, and stolen from for the last time.

"While you were busy training, using your Arcadian Guard techniques against one another, we were forced to stay on the sidelines, so you could grope us whenever you had the desire. While we brought you drinks and food, we were memorizing every move, and we practiced them every night while you slept."

She saw the exaggerated gulps of the men on their knees in the front row—fear from the men who could truly see the fire and insanity building in her eyes.

"We are every bit as skilled as you are, and I can promise you that if I ever see you so much as raise a hand to any of these women again, I will castrate you myself, using the dullest knife I can possibly find. Now, as I said before, if you don't want to serve me, you don't have to. Walk away if you'd like, but you'll find a knife in your back if you do."

To her surprise, several of them immediately lowered their eyes, showing the same subservience they had so recently forced from the women. Less to her surprise, there were men who tried to assert their dominance—prove they were stronger and faster—only to find their throats opened and bleeding out onto the ground beneath them.

As the remaining, undecided men looked on, seeing just how strong the women had become, and how fast and capable they were, they very quickly lowered their eyes as well.

Esmerelda smiled. "Ladies, they're all yours, to do with as you wish; just know that I expect them to live. We'll need their numbers in the days to come. Past that, do as you like." Satisfied, she turned and made her way out of the tent.

The Heights would be theirs, and she would be the queen that seized it.

CHAPTER THREE

For several days, Amelia had been working on something special for the city. She had set Waylon to one task, while the Academy was working on another. While the citizens were well aware something was going on, the majority had no idea what that was.

Nathaniel, the Cellan governor's son, had arrived, and was flourishing, just in the short time he had been there. Not only had he surpassed the basic magic class, thanks to his father teaching him along the way, he had tested in at the top of the intermediate magic class, and the top of the most advanced combat class. He had even offered to teach some of the combat class.

While he was still a student himself back in Cella, in Arcadia, he was more than qualified to teach the basic hand-to-hand combat courses now offered in the Academy. Even the civilians thought so.

Soon, the governor of Cella would be arriving to visit his son and Amelia and check on the city. While he had no claim and held no responsibility to Arcadia, he and Amelia had become great friends. She knew just how close he felt to the city, having fled there during his time of need and eventually fought for its freedom from the mystics.

She wanted to pay them back by doing more than just honoring their agreement. She wanted to do something special for him, for the Arcadian people, and put on a spectacle they could all enjoy together.

She had recently received notice from Arryn and Cathillian that they'd been successful in the forest. Now that the dark druids had been dealt with, the pair planned to head south to deal with the bandit problem. Amelia took delight in sharing this with the rearick brothers, who had been quite concerned for the safety of their people.

While Amelia hated sending Arryn and Cathillian to do her work—or at least, what she felt was her work—she took solace in knowing that the city needed her to stay close, able to react at a moment's notice if anything terrible were to happen.

As Amelia rounded the corner of a large, noble home, making her way toward the Boulevard, she smiled, and her breath caught in her throat as she took in the sights before her.

Children were running around and playing, spraying water at each other with small, pressurized devices. They screamed and laughed as they dodged one another's attacks.

The air had grown chilly as autumn began to set in. According to the rearick, it had already begun snowing in their small town in the mountains. Winter would soon be upon them again; Amelia couldn't believe just how much time had passed since their fight with Adrien.

She arrived at the Boulevard and saw a bright red ribbon, strung from the corner of one building to the corner of another across the street. She couldn't believe her eyes.

"Amelia," Marie greeted her, a large smile on her face. "The governor has arrived, and everyone is ready. What would you have me do?"

Amelia took in the chaos around them. Everyone from the

Academy was inside the Boulevard, awaiting instructions. Outside the red ribbon, the citizens waited to hear her news.

"Have the guards announce that the event is about to begin, then send Andrew to bring the governor back here; there's a spot reserved up front for him."

Marie smiled again and gave a curt nod before turning to do as she was asked. Delegation was something she was still learning, and it would take time for her to get the hang of it, but Amelia believed she was doing well enough.

The position of Chancellor suited her.

Ducking behind some buildings so she wasn't stopped by anyone, she snuck into the Boulevard. She moved past several houses before finding the group of students she was looking for.

Wives, mothers, and tailors in the city had worked hard to create a movable, breathable uniform that was easy for the students to train in. The guard had their own uniforms for training that differed from the ones they wore while on duty, but they were still rugged.

That had been in case the worst were to happen. If they were in a training session and there was an attack or anything that may require their immediate attention, they wouldn't have to change clothes, only grab weapons.

The Academy students wouldn't have anything like that to worry about. Therefore, their uniforms were lighter for easy movement and reduced heat.

Beginning students, who had very little to no former training at all, wore white.

The intermediate students, those that had previous training during the Battle for Arcadia, all wore brown.

The advanced students, those who had trained during the Battle for Arcadia and those who grew up in the Boulevard learning how to fight, all wore black.

"Is everything ready?" Nathaniel asked with a smile, straightening the top of his black uniform.

Amelia nodded. "Everything's ready, and the guards are rounding everyone up right now. Your father is on his way from the front gates. He came in later than I thought. I expected him to arrive last night, but I'm kind of glad he didn't; he might have caught wind of what was happening if he had arrived any sooner."

"I would have been just as disappointed as you. You know how hard I had to work to keep this from him? He has *excellent* intuition," he said.

Amelia laughed and nodded. "Oh, I bet he does. He's a very smart man. Okay, get everyone in line and ready. I'm going up to the front to watch for your father. Once he arrives, I'll begin my speech. Wait for my signal."

She began to make her way to the front of the Boulevard, making sure to stay behind the red line. She smiled back at everyone as they waved and smiled at her, some even shouting her name.

Within a few moments, the guard escort arrived at the front row with the governor of Cella in tow.

Once the governor was in place, Amelia gave him a nod of respect before raising her hands, signaling for everyone to quiet down. Everyone quickly acquiesced, and only the occasional cough or throat clear was audible.

"Before we kick things off, I would like to give a heartfelt welcome to the governor of Cella. Without him, today would not have been possible." Amelia's eyes lingered on the governor for a few moments as he smiled warmly in her direction. She returned his smile before once again addressing the crowd.

"As you all know, the governor has been kind enough to train our guards, which he continues to do. We are building a stronger city. Not only is our army strengthening, but so are our citizens.

"This red ribbon in front of me symbolizes the gateway to a brand-new life for every Boulevard native—and, in turn, for

Arcadia. Today, some of what has been taken from you is given back, so we can all move forward. Together!"

Everyone cheered for a moment before quieting again.

Amelia continued. "On behalf of our city, I say thank you to the governor of Cella for supplying the men, as well as some of the resources, necessary to rebuild. Thank you for defending us in our time of need, and for the training you have given our guards to defend us in the future. Thank you for lending a hand to make our city a more independent place."

The citizens erupted in cheers and screams of excitement. The governor seemed touched by the display, as he just smiled and waved to the people, a blush on his cheeks.

Amelia once again held up her hands, and the crowd quieted, though she could plainly see the excitement still on their faces. "Before I cut this ribbon, freeing you all to explore your new homes, I want to introduce everyone to the students of the Arcadian Academy, who show us just what equality looks like. What an *education* looks like in the *new* Arcadia!"

She began to clap, and everyone in the crowd followed suit as the students in the basic combat classes rounded the corner of the building. They were dressed in white and stepping out into the street, heading toward the ribbon. Behind them were the intermediate students, wearing brown, and then came those in the advanced class, clad in black.

Amelia stepped out of the way as the members of the basics class stepped up, walking in unison, and then broke off in pairs. The basics class was comprised mostly of noble students of various ages and Boulevard students in their early teens. This was the largest class.

Several parents in the audience gasped, their hands over their mouths as they smiled. Clearly, they hadn't expected what they were seeing; that meant the students had indeed kept their mouths shut. Amelia had gotten her wish for this all to be a surprise.

With a call from Nathaniel in the back, the students began to spar.

Because of their skill level, they were still unable to throw punches full force. They also did not have the ability to block yet. Because of that, their sparring looked more like a dance, a choreography of blows—one student throwing a punch as the other moved back, then rounding with a kick as the other ducked down.

Every movement had been well taught and was precise on both sides. With more practice, Amelia knew they would be able to speed those movements up and would soon be skilled enough to dodge a real punch and block a true kick.

Everyone clapped and cheered as the basics students backed away from one another and bowed to the crowd.

Next, the intermediate students stepped forward. The majority of this group were Boulevard students, so the crowd was even more engaged. The Bitch's Boulevard citizens loved and supported anything having to do with their kids being in the Academy. Seeing them not only as students, but as being accepted and treated as equal was new for them, and certainly something to be proud of.

Another call from Nathaniel, and the group began sparring, just as the basics class had, only these students were more disciplined.

A couple of punches landed, but for those who grew up in the Boulevard, things were tough, so its residents were tougher. The blows rolled right off like nothing happened. Amelia was impressed, and the crowd was even more so.

When those students backed away, and the students clad in black stepped up, all but a couple were Boulevard students. As the smallest group, the students broke off into three groups of three, engaging in group fighting instead of one-on-one combat.

Nathaniel led this group, and his father beamed with pride

from the front of the crowd. The governor, Amelia, and everyone else watched as the students began to fight one another.

It reminded Amelia quite a bit of the way the druids trained in the Dark Forest. They didn't have expert healers here, though there were a few people in the city who had learned the most basic version of the skill thanks to Arryn and Cathillian.

Because of that, they couldn't go as hard as the druids while training. Still, there were several punches thrown that landed hard.

The students moved quickly, jabbing and dodging one another's attacks. They used a mixture of street fighting and trained combat, though the skills they focused on in the Academy were for basic self-defense, so they could expertly take care of themselves.

Though it was new and impressive in the city, Amelia knew that the advanced class was essentially learning what they taught twelve-year-olds in the forest. While the students still had a lot to learn to become true warriors, they were definitely on the right path.

Nathaniel called out the end of the match, and everyone halted. The crowd once again screamed and cheered, the Boulevard residents cheering the loudest.

Amelia once again stepped forward and lifted her arms out, a wide smile on her face. As everyone began to quiet down, she spoke. "This was my first time seeing them as well, and I'm just as impressed as all of you. This is only the beginning; this is just what they have learned since our last battle. I wanted you to see exactly what we have been doing in the Academy, and what your children have been learning. They are our future.

"Without further introduction—as I know all of you are excited to go to your homes—I wish all of you the best, and sincerely thank you for your hard work and dedication to our city."

With that, Amelia pulled a knife from a small sheath on her

lower back and reached toward the ribbon. Before cutting, she looked up and said, "Once you have seen your homes, come out and join the fun. This celebration is *far* from over."

As Amelia finally cut the ribbon, colorful explosions filled the sky. Waylon had been given his own assignment for the occasion, and he absolutely delivered.

As everyone made their way into the Boulevard, Amelia saw the look of wonder on their faces. Everything had gone exactly as she had hoped—even better. She felt a sting in her eyes as she watched families hold each other and cry as they stepped over the threshold into their new homes.

Homes that had indoor plumbing. Running water. Magitech lighting.

They would be able to lead normal lives. Bathe and feed their children, have clean water to drink without fighting with the rest of the Boulevard over a single pump in the middle of the street.

Today was the day that Arcadia was officially reborn.

CHAPTER FOUR

Christopher held up his favorite sword, a katana that his late wife had commissioned for him. It had grown dull over the years, so he had spent the day sharpening the weapon. He wouldn't be able to use it during his current training, but he sure as hell planned to use it if there was ever another attack.

When Arryn had gone to get newly forged weapons from a man up north, she made a pit stop in Arcadia to retrieve his old swords for him. She had believed it would mean a lot to him and remind him a bit of who he was, but he doubted she knew just how much that act of kindness meant.

He sheathed the katana and set it aside, making his way out of his cabin and toward the trial pit. Today, he would be training with Ryel. It was the best decision for now, until he got his speed up.

"How are you feeling this morning?" Ryel asked.

Christopher smiled. "I'm feeling pretty good. Since the battle, I've been feeling quite a bit better about my abilities. Still, I don't feel it would be wise to go against Nika."

Ryel laughed. "I know what you mean. There are days when *I* don't even want to, and I feel like we are pretty evenly matched."

As they walked together, they passed the younger children making their way toward the Chieftain. He imagined they were off to learn how to heal and grow things within the forest. It seemed the Chieftain never stuck to one topic at a time; he taught them all.

As they made it to the pit, Christopher saw two students salute one another before backing away. Each of them had a combination of black eyes and bloodied noses and mouths, but they were still all smiles as they made their way out of the pit, where they would be healed.

Several students stepped back, smiling and bowing their heads in respect. While they didn't yet consider him one of their own, as they did Arryn, they did understand and have compassion for everything he had been through. They respected his ability to come out on the other side and maintain his humanity, though he felt his sanity wasn't yet fully in check.

Ryel tossed Christopher a blunted practice sword, holding one of his own and rotating it in the air at his side with only the flick of his wrist. Taking a deep breath, Christopher stepped forward, his eyes never leaving Ryel's.

The warrior gave a nod before lunging forward, Christopher immediately jumping back in response and swinging his sword. Steel clashing against steel as he successfully thwarted Ryel's attack.

It's slow, and it's sloppy, but I did it, he thought to himself. *Get your shit together and kick his ass. Your daughter can do it, so can you.*

Ryel lunged forward again, and this time Christopher leaned back, the sword narrowly missing his throat. As Ryel's swing missed, Christopher recoiled, dropping down to the ground to hit his opponent in the side of his dominant knee with the hilt.

As Ryel's knee gave out on him, Christopher whipped his blade around and had it at the warrior's throat before Ryel could even counter.

Both men smiled. Ryel nodded. "Nice shot. Glad to see you still have it in you."

Before Christopher could even thank him, Ryel lunged at him from his kneeling position to take a cheap shot. Christopher took a hard hit across the face, Ryel now on top of him with his fist pulled back and ready to deliver another.

Christopher slammed the hilt of his sword in Ryel's ribs, causing him to lean over in pain. As the warrior showed that brief moment of weakness, Christopher took advantage and threw his head forward, smashing Ryel's nose.

With a thrust of his hips, Christopher easily tossed Ryel off to take the dominant position, pulling the knife from the warrior's belt as they rolled before holding it to his throat.

Blood streamed down each side of Ryel's face, his eyes watering as a natural effect from his nose breaking. He nodded, and Christopher backed off, carefully handing the knife back to his opponent.

"I'm so sorry," Christopher said. "I don't know where that came from."

Ryel reached up, pinching each side of his nose and squeezing, the sound of bone fragments snapping and grinding back into place filling the small area between them as he healed himself.

Ryel shook his head. "Well, I think I learned something today."

"What's that?" Christopher asked, obvious worry on his face. He hadn't meant to break anything. He had been watching Arryn spar more and more, and had even snuck in to watch Nika train.

He didn't think watching would translate into movements, but somehow, he managed to take Ryel not once but twice. While he felt terrible for breaking the warrior's nose, he felt triumphant that he was able to do it.

"I think it's time for you to move on," Ryel said before standing.

Christopher looked at him in confusion as he followed suit, standing. "I don't understand."

"I think it's time we let Nika get a hold of you. You've clearly learned a lot more in your short time here than we anticipated. Then again, you had prior training, so this is probably partly due to that, and partly you being an incredibly fast learner. Just like your daughter," Ryel said.

Christopher smiled. He was supposed to be a role model for his daughter, not the other way around, but that was just how it was. He could argue it in his head, telling himself that he was wrong for allowing that to be, but he didn't care. It was just the way their lives turned out, and having a strong daughter who was capable of not only taking care of herself, but of everyone around her…

Well, he couldn't have asked for anything more.

Except for a higher pain tolerance. Because despite what Ryel thought, Nika was far scarier than he was.

"Sending me to the Wolf is punishment for breaking your nose, isn't it?" Christopher asked.

Ryel smiled. "'Wolf'. I can't tell you just how appropriate that name is for her. And yes, this is definitely repayment for you breaking my nose."

Christopher laughed, but it was quickly extinguished the moment Nika walked up with a smile that was a bit too broad.

"Did I just overhear that I'm getting a new student?" Nika asked, mischief in her expression.

Christopher nodded with a bit of hesitation. "Ryel thinks I'm ready."

Nika looked at Ryel and laughed harder than Christopher had ever seen. "Aw, poor baby. I think he just got his little feelings hurt because the man that's been stuffed in a cave for a decade whipped his ass. That's okay, Chris. Looks like you needed a real man to teach you, anyway. I'll be that man."

She smiled again and gave him a wink before turning and walking away. Christopher and Ryel looked at one another, Ryel shaking his head.

"You realize sh—" Christopher began.

"Mmhmm. Yep. She's gonna kill you. Don't worry. I'll tell Arryn you love her."

———

THE SUN GLARED off the gentle waves rolling in along the Farriage Coast. The water had a beautiful aquamarine color, allowing it to cast off the sun's rays, making the sea look as though it twinkled.

Brann smiled as he stepped forward, placing his slightly webbed toes in the water, wiggling them around as they pushed further into the sand. He sighed in contentment, taking another step forward, and then another.

Brann's people had lived in and by the water for a very long time. His grandparents were among the first settlers there. After traveling all over during the madness, there wasn't much land available that wasn't taken over by the remnant.

Those beasts had ruined everything for many people, forcing them to scatter to wherever they might find a plot of land large enough to survive on, no matter how small it may be.

His family, however, had gone to the ocean. There was absolutely nothing they couldn't get from the water. Over the years, with the magic that had grown inside of them, their bodies had begun to change.

Their fingers and toes were webbed halfway up, allowing them to swim faster than a normal human, but still allow them the ability to use common tools. Their ears had grown tighter against their heads, as well—not quite flat, but certainly set at a different angle than on any other human they had ever come across.

While in the water, they each had the ability to regulate their body temperature, allowing them to swim even when the water was cold. That was more than likely due to the fact that the Daoine people spent the majority of their days in the sea.

Brann dove in, immediately swimming farther out and heading downward. Off in the distance, he could see the dolphins playing under the water. Every day he paid them a visit, swimming with them and playing with them. Several had swum very deep, two of them now racing for the surface.

He knew if he were to watch from above, he would see a beautiful aerial display before their long, pointed noses broke the surface of the water again as they dove.

Brann's eyes glowed a beautiful aquamarine shade, as he moved his hands through the water, pulling oxygen from it to create an air pocket around his head. He inhaled deep before letting it go, propelling himself forward.

The magic flowed through his body, allowing his legs to propel him faster than any of the dolphins could swim.

Though the dolphins and whales had become accustomed to the water dwellers' presence years ago—at the very least for as long as he had been alive—it had only been in the last two years that he had surpassed his loved ones to become truly accepted as one of the pod.

While Druids were capable of speaking to land animals, because of their magic and because of living among them in the forest, the water dwellers had never been able to communicate with the sea creatures. His mother had always said it was more than likely because fish weren't mammals, so their brains were different.

But Brann had noticed a change in the dolphins, in the way they interacted with him. Deep down, he knew it was because of his persistence to learn when his family hadn't truly cared to. It didn't hurt that dolphins were intelligent creatures.

A shadow fell over him as he swam, and he suddenly felt cold. Dolphins and whales frequented the very water he swam in, but sharks also came. His parents always told he and his siblings to be careful, because the sharks had been changing their migratory patterns for quite some time.

While they preferred sea lions and other such creatures, a human was certainly not off the menu.

With his heart racing, and his adrenaline pumping, his need for oxygen came much faster than usual. He surrounded his head once again with a bubble, inhaling deep as he looked around. His magic began to crawl across his skin, ready for whatever might come.

Then he heard a familiar call.

He turned abruptly to see a nearly full-grown, but rather small, dolphin stopping short of him, a fish in his mouth. It was Finn, the first dolphin to have accepted him as more than another presence in the water.

Finn opened his mouth, dropping the dead fish for Brann to take. The dolphin often tried to feed Brann, providing him with fish, which the twelve-year-old boy always accepted. Brann lifted the fish to his mouth, taking a squishy bite out of the belly.

Though he preferred his fish cooked, eating them raw was normal among his people because they spent so much time swimming in the water.

After Brann took his third bite while slowly swimming along, he gave the rest back to Finn, who happily finished it off. The dolphin then darted forward, spinning around and swimming straight for the surface, his deformed tail fin moving him at an impressive speed.

It always warmed Brann's heart to see the two-year-old calf swim as fast and with as much excitement as he did. Finn wasn't born with that deformity, and Brann would never forget how he got it.

As usual, he had been swimming close to the dolphins' play area. He had seen a female's belly swelling more and more every day, and stayed close, wanting to watch the birth out of curiosity.

While it was the most disgusting thing he had ever seen, it was also the most beautiful. A perfect, dark gray, male dolphin had been born. But sharks had smelled the blood and came to attack.

The newborn wasn't able to swim fast enough to get away, and a shark snatched him by the tail. He had only landed a single bite, when several dolphins attacked from either side, ramming the shark in the gills with their long noses.

Brann, disobeying everything his parents had ever told him, called on his magic and swam as fast as he possibly could. The calf could no longer move his tail, not that it would have helped him anyway. He was sinking fast, and Brann knew he would soon drown if he didn't save him.

He managed to grab the newborn, cradling him tight against his body as he used his magic to propel himself through the water. He went straight up, narrowly missing a chomp from a great white, before the other dolphins swarmed that one, as well.

When Brann breached the surface, he brought the calf up, allowing him to breathe. Once he was certain the dolphin had taken a breath or two, he surrounded its blowhole with a large bubble of oxygen—hoping his magic would work on the mammal—and swam toward the shore.

When Brann had gotten close, he carefully laid the calf on the sand in water that was just deep enough to cover his small body. Blood poured out of his little tail, and tears filled Brann's eyes.

He had watched the mother carry the calf for a full year, and now the baby was dying. He reached out, putting pressure on the tail, but it was too badly mangled. The blood continued to flow. The fins were still intact, but a mess.

He felt the magic swelling around him, and he pushed it forward, not knowing what else to do. Mother dolphins were terribly protective, and even though he had tried save the baby, he knew the mother would be devastated.

But then, the bleeding stopped.

He looked down to see that the wounds had closed. The magic he had felt moving through him, the heat he'd felt growing in his hands, had closed the wound. It certainly wasn't pretty; the tail fin was still mangled, scarred, but learning to move in his mother's current, the baby would grow stronger until he would finally be able to swim.

After the immediate threat of the sharks was gone, the dolphins came as close to the shore as they could.

Brann picked up the calf and swam out to the pod. To his surprise, the mother seemed very grateful, despite the damage that had been done. While he knew she would be relieved the calf hadn't died, he was worried she might not understand that he had tried to save the little guy.

But from that day forward, Brann had been accepted as one of them, and had appropriately named the calf 'Finn'.

A loud cry from the pod now alerted Brann, pulling him out of his thoughts as he played with Finn underwater. The dolphins were swimming erratically, and Finn's mother was coming to retrieve her calf.

Brann surrounded his head once more with air as he looked around for danger. Another shadow fell over him, and he immediately looked up.

Thinking about Finn and the way they had met had distracted him so much that he hadn't noticed the storm that had begun to coalesce over the water, nor the large ship that now floated well over his head.

Dolphins were highly intelligent animals and were used to seeing boats and ships out on the water. But they could also sense danger from a mile away, as well as sense magic—something his parents had told him long ago.

Brann could also sense magic, and there was a lot of it coming from the bow of that ship.

If the occupants of the ship were strong enough to call storms and scare away the dolphins, who were used to seeing magic on a daily basis, exactly who were they, and what could they possibly want from his people?

CHAPTER FIVE

Selena stood at the bow of her ship, staff held firm. The tip of the staff was planted in a cup of seawater, allowing her to channel the power of the sea itself. Storm Callers had a reputation for ruling whatever body of water they sailed across.

Each Caller was put through trials and trained rigorously throughout their life; only when they had proven themselves to be the best of the best were they given an assignment on a ship.

To even be considered, each potential Storm Caller would be thrown into the sea, while another Caller would stand on land, calling forth a hellacious storm. The waters would become dangerous at best, but deadly for many. If the sea swallowed the contender, their training was obviously not yet finished if they survived.

Pitted against a senior Storm Caller's magic, only recruits strong enough to calm the waters and swim to shore would be bestowed the sought-after title of Caller.

How well they performed during their trial would determine what ship they were assigned to, and if they would even be chosen right away.

Selena was one of the best. Her training had always been

strong, and she was certainly one of the most gifted. But on her training day, a moment of distraction allowed her to be swallowed by the angry waters. She nearly drowned, but at the last moment, overcame her fear and took control.

Though she pulled herself to the surface and managed to swim the rest of the way to the shore, the damage had already been done, and she was passed up in favor of those who she considered much weaker than herself.

She worked harder than ever, rebuilding her reputation, allowing her fury at her own weakness to drive her. That determination got her noticed by Captain Tor. While he didn't have room on his own ship for her, a new ship had been crafted within his fleet, and he offered her a position on it.

Being associated with the captain was an honor above all. Even though she wouldn't be Calling on his ship, she excitedly accepted the opportunity to be accepted as part of his fleet.

When he was killed by his own people, the very people that had claimed to love and adore him—in his hometown of Holdgate, no less—she and her captain had decided to carry on his work.

There was still much to be done, and the Storm Raiders would continue on in Captain Tor's honor. Selena was eternally grateful to him for the opportunities he had given her. As far as she was concerned, she would never be done doing his work.

She had received word there was a growing village down south, with weapons that had been newly engineered, and were promised to be stronger than anything anyone had ever seen.

Granted, that information had come from a drunk man who had purchased such a weapon—negating the idea that it would be unique among people in that area.

But still, Selena and Captain Seth planned to sail out and explore other areas, far away from the village. In those places, their weapons certainly wouldn't have been seen. They would be unique and powerful among those people.

They could rip apart any village they chose and take whatever they wanted. No one could stop them.

"Do you see that?" the captain asked.

Selena nodded, a smile on her face. "Where do you think I'm headed?"

Captain Seth laughed. "I suppose I shouldn't be surprised. Do you think we might find weapons there?"

With little hesitation, she said, "No. I highly doubt the people here have much of anything. The village we are looking for is farther south than this, and they use strong tents for housing. Not shitty houses built out of rock and whatever junk pieces of wood they can find."

The captain shrugged. "No matter. If they have anything, we'll find it. Bring her in."

Selena smiled. "Yes, sir."

Her eyes flashed greenish blue as thunder boomed overhead. She gripped her staff tighter as she felt the magic flow through her. The wind changed direction then, aiming them directly for the village.

Though she couldn't hear them over the sounds of the crashing waves against the ship and the loud wind whipping around her, she saw people racing out of the water and onto dry land. She was caught off guard by just how many people were swimming, especially in early fall—the waters were far too cold.

As they got close, the crew began to fill the boats on the side of the ship and lower themselves down. Selena grabbed her staff and made for the one designated for her. It would stay on the water, far enough away she could channel the power of the sea, but close enough that she could effectively use her magic.

"Go, go, go!" Seth shouted. "No mercy."

The men and women screamed out in excitement at the captain's words, as Selena used her abilities to push their boats toward shore. It didn't take long for her to find her own position, and for the Raiders to reach land. Within seconds, they had weapons drawn and were rushing the village.

Now that she was much closer, she could hear the screams of terror. The villagers ran, but not many tried to fight; it was obvious the village was full of peaceful people.

Oh, well. Too bad for them, she thought. *They deserve to die for their stupidity.*

Her eyes flashed again as lightning began to web across the sky.

BRANN SAW the ship as he rose to the surface. It was heading toward his village, but not directly. The angle was such that it appeared it could turn away at any moment. Unfortunately, that didn't last.

Thunder cracked overhead, and the wind began to blow from the east, turning the ship directly toward his village. Brann's eyes widened just before they flashed aquamarine. He dove under the water, where he was fastest, and swam for shore.

Once there, he ran as hard as he could, hoping to reach the rear of his village before the invaders did. He knew getting caught would result in a very quick and, more than likely, painful death.

He hid behind a small cottage at the back of his village. Their homes were small and modest, quickly built and easily maintained. They didn't need much room, as most of their time was spent outdoors or in the sea. Still, their homes held all of their belongings, what little they had.

He could smell smoke and quickly saw the plumes rising overhead. Those men were setting his village on fire, and there was nothing he could do about it.

He heard the screams of terrified villagers. Risking a peek around the corner of the cottage, he saw for the first time exactly what his grandparents and the rest of the original settlers had feared most.

He'd heard tales of the remnant, and knew what they looked like. These were men. Humans. But they were not much different.

His gut twisted as he saw a young woman running in his direction, heading for the end of the village, only to be impaled by a spear. It had been thrown from some distance behind her, by one of the biggest men Brann had ever seen.

The girl grunted, almost gurgled, then the sound was cut off as she fell forward from the force. Her eyes were wide, her jaw slack. Brann saw no pain on her face, only the shock and fear that she had felt in her last moments.

Anger swelled inside of him. The man—the *murderer*—almost growled, a dark smile spreading across his face as he locked eyes with Brann. As Brann stared into the eyes of that man, knowing for the first time the true cruelty the world was capable of, he thought again of the shark.

The shark, he realized, wasn't so bad. It didn't go after the calf because it was an evil creature. That shark had gone after the calf because it had smelled the blood and had followed its instincts. It was simply surviving.

The man now approaching him with a smile that reminded him of the jagged grin of the great white, did not kill for necessity. He did not kill on instinct. He did not kill to survive.

He killed because he enjoyed it.

"Come here, boy," the man said as he pulled his spear free from the young woman that now lay dead on the ground. "I've got something for you. She liked it. See? She's speechless." The man laughed, and Brann grew even angrier.

As he stepped out from behind the cottage, the man's murderous eyes widened.

"Not gonna run?" he asked.

Brann slowly shook his head, his fists clenched tight. His head was angled down, but his aqua-colored eyes were staring straight into those of the bastard standing before him.

"Impressive. Stupid, but impressive," the man said with another demented smile.

Brann's eyes flashed even brighter as his hands went out to his sides. He moved his hands in flat circles, as if on a table before him. The Raider's smile faded as he began to cough.

Brann drew nearly all of the moisture out of the air surrounding the man, making it very difficult for him to breathe. He then shoved his hands downward, forcing all the water into the ground around the man.

As large as the man was, he immediately began to sink into the softened sand, and fear spread across his face.

Not enough.

Brann continued to work, pulling more and more moisture out of the air and forcing it downward as the man struggled, tripping as he tried to free himself of the quicksand.

Now that he was flat, Brann was able to make even quicker work of him, forcing the wet sand to swallow him up to the shoulders. Still, he couldn't bring himself to deliver the final blow. Even after seeing what he had, he was still only a boy.

Instead, he left it for the gods to decide. If the man struggled and killed himself, it would be the gods who willed it.

Brann ducked behind the cottage again, choosing his next path carefully. He needed to find his parents and baby sister. In his village, the elderly stayed in homes with children who were too young to swim in the sea, and who hadn't yet been taught magic.

His young sister was a very strong swimmer at four years old, but still didn't have her magic. He was five when he learned his, so he knew she wasn't long off. But she was still too young to escape to the water in hopes of fleeing.

He found his way to a cottage that was just a few down from his family's. He looked around the corner, his eyes widening as he saw the smoke billowing from his home. His heart began to race, all sense of self-preservation gone as he ran for the tiny house.

As he approached, he saw his sister climbing out of the window, tears streaming down her dirty face. She fell to the ground, coughing and clutching at her chest. He ran to her, pulling her to his chest as he wrapped her legs around his waist, and turned to run.

"It's okay, Sasha," he said, not certain he believed that himself. "I've got you."

"Mommy and daddy…" the little girl said, sniffling as she spoke.

His heart sank as he carefully made his way around the cottage. He could hear the screams of death all around him. He could smell burning meat, and knew that it wasn't animal he was smelling. All he wanted to do was collapse, curl up in a ball, and cry his eyes out.

But he couldn't.

"There you are!" a man growled, chilling Brann to the bone.

He turned his head and saw a man coming for them. It appeared that he had come out of the cottage. Without a doubt, Brann knew that his parents were dead. They had died to save his sister.

He sure as hell wasn't about to let them die in vain.

He set his sister down on the ground. "Close your eyes, Sasha," he told her.

"Aw, isn't that sweet?" the man said from behind him. "Doesn't matter. You'll be dead soon, just like your parents in that little hut there, and then we'll be back on our way south. You'll never be thought of again."

Brann stood and turned, knowing that this time he didn't have a choice. If it came down to himself or that man, he would have to choose himself. His sister had no one left and would certainly die without him.

Brann didn't know how to fight, but when the man came at him with the spear, he was surprised that he had incredibly quick reflexes. All his time in the water, playing with the dolphins had made him stronger and faster on land.

The spear was thrust forward, and Brann easily spun out of the way. His eyes flashed aquamarine, and he became very aware that he had used far too much magic in the last fight. This time, he would have to do the one thing he knew he could do but had desperately tried to avoid.

As the man thrust forward again, Brann spun out of the way, rolling to the ground and coming up on his knees. He lifted his hands into the air, just as he would if he were pulling oxygen from the water to create a bubble around his head. Then he spun them as if he were circling them around the ball, and water was pulled from the air to engulf the man's head.

The man's eyes went wide, and he very quickly fell to his knees, scratching and clawing at the water, trying to get away from it.

But Brann held strong.

Looking over at his sister, he saw that not only were her eyes closed tight, but her little hands covered them as well, her knees pulled tight into her chest as she trembled in fear. He wished that he could close his own eyes. He wished that he didn't have to see what he was about to do, but if he closed his eyes for even a second, the spell would weaken, and the man would get free.

Instead, he allowed the death of his parents and the need to save his sister fill him with strength.

Brann watched the man grow weaker and weaker, until finally he fell forward on the ground. Brann knew not to let the water go; the man had simply passed out. He wasn't dead yet.

Brann's chest heaved a bit, as tears filled his eyes, and he sniffed as he fought back the urge to sob. He could feel the man dying.

And then, it was done. Whatever life essence had been there before, wasn't there now.

Brann knew he'd caused that, but he couldn't dwell on that now.

"Bubby?" His sister's voice was terrified and weak. "Bubby, are you still there? Please don't be dead, too. I can't look."

His heart ached at Sasha's words, and he quickly dropped his magic and rushed over to her.

"I'm right here. I'm not going anywhere." He picked her up and wrapped her around him, just as he had before. "Be very quiet. I have to get us to the water. We have family down south, and we need to warn them."

CHAPTER SIX

"So, what you're saying is, you'd totally be open to a fling with Sam if you two were the last people on Irth," Arryn said to Cathillian.

Samuel groaned. "I don't like this game."

"Oh, come on. It's not *that* bad," Cleo said. "He's certainly the prettiest man *I've* ever seen."

Cathillian turned and smiled with excitement. "*Thank* you, Cleo. At least *someone* thinks so." He turned to Arryn. "And that's *not at all* what I said. You know you're the only person I could stand to irritate for eternity."

"Stop trying to get out of this so easily," Arryn said, on the verge of laughing. "The rules were simple. You had to choose between spending a night with Talia or spending the night with Samuel. You clearly chose Sam. I mean, Talia was an evil, horrible, piece of shit, but all that aside, she was an attractive female. Don't get mad at me, I didn't make up the rules."

Another groan came from the rearick. "That was a damned setup if I ever saw one. Besides... We're supposed ta be on a serious journey here. Do ye really have nothin' better ta do than pick on me?"

Cathillian let out a *hmmph*. "Maybe I just prefer quality over looks. Is that so shocking?" he asked Arryn. After a brief pause, he turned back to Samuel. "No offense."

The rearick rolled his eyes. "None taken. We ain't a pretty lot."

Arryn opened her mouth to speak, planning to crack a joke about Cathillian's obvious narcissism and why his choice was so funny, but Samuel interrupted. "Ye know what? Since all ye bastards 're out ta make a joke outta little ol' me, and Cathillian here was willin' ta choose me in that rotten scenario, I'd have te say I'd accept. 'Cause if I was left with any o' *yer* mean asses, the human species would *still* die out. At least with him, I'd be respected. Yer a bunch o' assholes."

Arryn and the twins laughed at being called assholes.

"Ha! See? Quality. Don't worry, Sam. I got your back," Cathillian said.

Bast laughed really hard. "*We know*! That's why we're laughing so hard!"

"I hate you all," Cathillian said.

Arryn was about to respond again, but silhouettes in the distance caught her attention.

She and her group had been traveling for a couple of days by the time they approached the main road that led from Craigston to Arcadia. The road was mostly frequented by rearick headed to the city to deliver amphorald crystals—stones that gave power to weapons, lights, and many other things—as well as anyone outside of the city who might be able to buy the products. It wasn't uncommon to see travelers on the road.

Before the bandits had invaded the Valley, the main road had been the safest way to travel, for rearick and farmers alike. Farmers and crafters would take their goods to Arcadia and sell them to shops or passersby. It was how they made their money. But as of late, people were far too terrified to travel the road, because of the dangers that lurked in the shadows.

As Arryn watched the small group of people heading toward

the city, she said, "Well, that's a good sign. It seems people are braving the road again."

Snow grumbled beneath her, and Arryn's brows furrowed. She looked forward, squinting as she tried to inspect the travelers from such a distance.

"What is it?" Cathillian asked.

"Snow says she can smell blood on those people," she replied. "Blood can mean anything, though. I can't tell from here if they're hostile or friendly."

"If they were hostile, I'd think they'd be travelin' off ta the side o' the road, an' not directly on it," Samuel said.

Arryn only nodded her head, sending a silent message to Snow to pick up the pace. Without hesitation, the tiger acquiesced. Within moments, the travelers in question became much more visible, and Arryn could see adults in the front and back of their party, with children in the middle.

They were traveling as a pride of lions would, with the strongest around the perimeter, and the youngest and weakest toward the center.

"They're innocents," Arryn called back, Snow running even faster.

Arryn could hear horse hooves thundering behind her, and knew the others were racing to keep pace. Within moments, they reached the travelers, and Arryn was met with a terrible sight.

"Holy shit," she said under her breath as Snow slowed to a stop several yards ahead of them. Or at least, she *thought* she had spoken under her breath; in fact, her volume was quite loud enough for the travelers to hear.

The adults immediately looked terrified, no doubt worried about the intentions of the people in front of them. Not to mention the white tiger the size of the Clydesdale, and the other tiger—though only a cub—who was now equal in size and weight to a full-grown female.

"Please don't be afraid," Arryn said, trying to calm them. The adults looked at one another, the dirt and blood on their faces only accentuating the fear in their eyes. "I want to help you. If any of you are injured, we can heal you. Three of us are druids."

Speaking the word 'druids' seemed to draw more fear. It was obvious they lived outside of the city, and only had heard tales to fuel their imaginations.

At that moment, Arryn wished she had paid more attention at the Temple. A bit of compulsion could go a long way in this situation.

"We have nothing. Please, don't hurt the children." A mother stood out from the group, tears in her eyes but determination on her face. "They took everything. We have nothing left to give you."

Arryn sighed, her heart breaking for the people in front of her. "Snow," she said softly.

The tiger lowered to the ground, even laying her head down on her paws as Arryn slowly climbed off. Out of her peripheral, Arryn saw Dante also lowering to the ground, after a mild grumble from his mother. Corrine stepped forward, her eyes flashing neon green as she reached a hand out.

The mother's eyes widened, and then immediately closed as she inhaled deeply, her brows pushing together. At that moment, Arryn noticed a large wet spot on the side of her tunic. The cloth was dark gray in color, so the black spot simply looked like a shadow.

It was blood.

Corrine dropped her hand, her eyes turning back to their normal emerald color, before a small, subtle smile spread across her lips. Arryn's eyes turned from her adolescent companion to the woman, whose eyes now opened.

Arryn felt pride swell inside of her as she realized that Corrine was mastering her healing abilities. The polar opposite of the people she had come from, she was the light among the darkness. Alaric had been capable of killing from a distance, but it was Corrine's strength to heal.

A power she had discovered when she was faced with losing the person that meant the most to her: Arryn.

"We really don't mean you any harm," Corrine said. "If you'll give her a chance, Arryn can probably help you. Maybe even set things on a path to make things right."

The woman wiped her tears away, smearing the blood and filth on her face in the process. She nodded toward Corrine before turning to Arryn. "I guess you're Arryn?"

Arryn nodded. "I am. As you probably suspect, we're from the Dark Forest. We're heading south of the Heights, hoping to stop a large village of bandits from terrorizing the Valley."

The adults in the group all looked at one another before looking back to her. "You know about them?" a man asked.

Arryn nodded again. "Unfortunately, we have quite a bit of experience with them. They have been terrorizing the area and killing many friends of my rearick companion back there. We fought a great number of them in the forest several days ago, and even killed their leader. Unfortunately, there are many more to deal with, south of the Heights."

Above them, Echo's screech filled the air. The travelers' eyes widened again, no doubt surprised to see yet another oversized animal.

To her left, Cathillian stepped forward. "I'm going to send my familiar, Echo, to Arcadia with you. She will make sure nothing happens to you. I assure you, she is more than capable of defending you."

"How long ago were you attacked?" Samuel asked, obvious anger in his voice.

"Not long. Within the last couple of hours," one of the villagers said. "Our village is small. Probably the smallest one in the Valley. There ain't really much left, but you'll find it about a mile and a half southeast of here. They took what they wanted, slaughtered our animals, and burned the rest."

Arryn gripped her fists tight, rage welling in her chest. It was basically the same thing that had happened to the old woman and her sons up north. The bandits had injured the cows badly enough that they would suffer hard until they died, and even killed one of the old woman's sons.

It seemed that the murderers and thieves liked to completely destroy the lives of whoever they affected.

"Do you think we can catch them?" Arryn asked Cathillian and Samuel.

"Are they on foot?" Samuel asked the travelers.

Several of them nodded before the mother that Corrine had healed spoke. "They were. That doesn't mean that they still are, but when they left the village, they were on foot and headed south."

Samuel shook his head. "Craigston has to be on high alert right now. There's no way the bandits would risk going directly through the town. If they're heading directly south, there has to be a path leading up the mountain and around Craigston. Still, I don't know how they could manage. That side is pretty much impossible to climb."

"They used magic when they set our houses on fire," the mother said. "I don't know if that helps or not."

Arryn nodded. "It does. That means they are physical magic users. They were once Arcadian Guard, so they are highly trained in hand-to-hand combat, as well as in magic. Samuel, if you're right, and that side of the mountain is damn near impossible to climb, I'm betting they use teleportation. I highly doubt they could teleport themselves and the horses up the mountainside, though, so I'm willing to bet they are still on foot."

Samuel smiled. "Then that means we can definitely catch them, lass."

Cathillian sighed and smiled as he nodded. "Oh, I know what

this means. Corrine, you and I are on healing duty. We can't let Arryn use any of her magic; I have a feeling she's gonna need it."

Corrine didn't seem to mind. She smiled as she stepped forward, excited to help the others. The villagers stepped aside, pointing out those that were injured in their group.

The mother spoke again. "How fast can you travel?"

Arryn looked down at Snow and smiled. "Normally, tigers can run about forty miles an hour. Snow is much bigger and much faster than a normal tiger; her son is, as well."

The mother stepped forward, briefly looking around to make sure that no one could hear her. "Nothing will bring back what we've lost. It was more than just our homes and a few lives. We lost our sense of security and safety on our own land. I didn't want to say this in front of the rest, but if you think you can catch them, make them suffer for what they did to my children."

Arryn nodded. "This is what we do. I promise you... one way or another... We will find them, and we will stop them from doing this to anyone else."

The woman nodded, pausing for a moment before she said, "The big one—Jack or John or something like that—he stole a necklace that my mother gave me as a child before she died. It's a golden cross. It's hundreds of years old and has been passed down from generation to generation. If you can find a way to get that back to me, I'll know it's been done."

With a smile, Arryn reached out and squeezed the woman's hand. "Follow Echo to Arcadia. You'll have your necklace back before you know it. Rest assured, I keep my promises... and I promise there will be a great deal of pain involved for them."

CHAPTER SEVEN

After healing everyone who had sustained injuries, Echo was sent along with the group of travelers, while Arryn and her own group rushed south. As expected, Snow, Dante, and Maia were the fastest. Bast and Cleo both told Arryn and Cathillian to go ahead. They would stay behind with Samuel.

Along with Corrine, they raced southeast for the mountains in hopes of catching the men. As expected, two hours on foot wasn't much time to get a lot of distance, so they were easily able to find the bastards. With Snow and Dante's keen sense of smell, they found the men heading toward the first tall rock.

Just as Samuel had said, upon inspection, Arryn could tell it was absolutely impossible to climb the mountain by normal means. While an experienced climber could do so with the right tools, she knew those men weren't carrying that much equipment.

Though each of the six men had a rather large bag on their back, the necessary climbing aids would have weighed them down so much, and taken up so much room in their packs, that it would be impossible for them to make off with the goods they had stolen.

Two of the men suddenly disappeared, reappearing twenty or thirty feet higher up the mountain. They were smart; instead of taking long jumps, exhausting themselves in the process, they were teleporting only a small distance. Arryn herself had done that when coming down from the mountains in the Frozen North.

Without Arryn having to ask her to, Snow sped up, racing past the others and heading toward her mark.

The men turned and saw the tiger and woman coming for them. Though they didn't seem to be scared, evidence to that having come in the form of a loud laugh from one or two of the men, the party still made sure they were out of reach.

Arryn only smiled. "Get back here, so I can kick your asses!" she called out.

Again, she was met with laughter.

"I'm not joking!" she said as she stepped up to the edge of mountain. "If I have to come up there after you, you're not gonna like what happens. Well, you're not going to anyway, but you'll like it even less."

She could hear them up there, talking to one another, and she was relatively certain she heard a condescending remark or two at her expense.

She sighed.

Her eyes flashed green as she called on her magic. Though she could sense how good or bad a person was within close proximity, these men were certainly too far away for her to do so. Before she ended the lives of six strangers, she needed to know they were the ones she was looking for.

Although, even if they weren't the ones she was looking for, they could still use a good punch or two to teach them some manners.

As she reached out, sensing them as an animal would a human they had just met, she was overcome with a cold sensation. It felt like death. They were absolutely the men she was looking for, and she had a promise to keep.

"I have a message for you, from the people who lived in that village you destroyed," Arryn shouted.

She heard an audible groan from above as the men continued to climb. They only had a few feet to go before they would be forced to teleport again. One of them grunted as he reached his platform and straightened himself and the pack on his back. When he turned, there was a wide smile on his face as he looked down at her from over forty feet up the mountain.

"What was that? Did you say you have a message, *sweetheart?*" he asked.

Arryn smiled, her eyes flashing black, as her magic surrounded her before imploding. She vanished, reappearing right next to the man who had just spoken down to her. His eyes widened as he turned, jumping back and nearly falling.

Her hand shot out, grabbing him by the shirt, and pulled him flush against her. "They said to die screaming, you murderous piece of shit."

With that, she whipped her hand out, using a bit of telekinesis to aid her movement as she threw him off the side of the mountain. Looking to either side of her, she saw two men on one side and three on the other at various heights, and watched as their eyes turned black.

Arryn felt the swell of her magic around her again as it imploded, teleporting her from where she stood, to the flat rock that the man the farthest to the left stood on.

A fireball that had been meant for her hit the man several yards to her right as she thrust a knee into the gut of the man next to her before pulling her blade free and jabbing it in the side of his throat. With little effort, she pulled the knife from the side of his neck and threw him over the edge of the mountain.

She turned around just in time to see more fireballs heading for her. Her arm shot out, forming a magical shield in front of her, only barely catching the fire as it exploded.

Black green bled into her irises as she lifted her left hand, swiping it hard to the right. A hard wind blew, smashing the last three men against the hard rocks, the bones in their skulls crushing in the process.

Two of them fell from their various heights, one tumbling all the way down to the base of the mountain, while the other only fell part of the way down. The third dropped right where he stood, his platform large enough to hold his collapsed body.

She took a deep breath, steadying herself. She knew she only had one last teleportation in her, but she had to use it. After teleporting over to the man that remained on the mountain, she checked his entire body and even the bag. There were women's belongings in there, jewelry and things of that sort, but nothing resembling the cross that had been described to her.

The sound of footsteps echoed from below. She looked down to see Bast, Cleo, and Samuel arriving.

Ah, just in time.

"Hey!" she called down. "I'm kind of stranded up here. Can I get a little help from one of you lovely ladies?"

She didn't feel completely depleted, but knowing they could run into another battle at any moment, she felt it was necessary to save whatever energy she had left.

Bast and Cleo both jumped down from their horses, stepping forward and moving in tandem—as they often did. Their fists shot forward, and the ground directly under Arryn started shaking, forcing her to kneel. The twins' palms flattened as they lifted, and the rock breaking away quickly descended to the ground below.

"Thanks!" Arryn said, stepping off her platform.

As she walked toward Cathillian, he stared at her with a knowing expression. Corrine looked excited about what had just taken place. Every time she saw Arryn's magic, she seemed enthralled.

"What?" she asked Cathillian.

He just shook his head, smiling at her. "Oh, nothing. You're just my hero, that's all."

She rolled her eyes. "Oh, shut it and help me check the bodies. I have a necklace to find and a message to deliver once we get to Craigston."

CHAPTER EIGHT

The sky was a beautiful shade of blue, only a speckling of the purest white clouds above them. Mariana held tight to her staff, her eyes focused and flashing as she called on just enough magic to summon the wind to fill their sails.

They were getting close, she could feel it. She wasn't exactly sure how far ahead of them the Storm Raiders were, but the sea seemed almost angry. The marine life in the area was disturbed, almost frightened by the sight of the ship, something they more than likely saw on a day-to-day basis.

While that wasn't evidence of the Raiders' proximity, it was certainly enough to fuel her and her magic.

A familiar scent filled her nose, and she looked to the right to see one of the crew offering her a mug of ale. "You've worked hard today," Ronald said. "We've traveled much faster than anticipated. I think it's safe for you to take a little bit of a break."

Mariana opened her mouth to object, but a guilty look crossed Ronald's face. "Also," he said, "Captain says so."

She sighed, smiling as she rolled her eyes. Reaching out, one hand still on the staff, she used the other to graciously take the mug, quickly chugging it before handing it over.

"Thank you," she said. "You tell Captain Veren that I said if he has orders for me to take breaks, he should deliver them himself. Not that I don't mind seeing that precious face of yours, Ron."

She smiled, and he shrank back a little, shyly smiling as he looked down. It was obvious that he had at least a small fraction of interest in her, though she wasn't sure if it was a physical interest or an emotional one. Still, she knew the comment made him feel good, and he was a kind man who helped everyone onboard.

"Well, between the two of us, I think he was a bit scared to tell you himself. He knows what this assignment means to you."

She laughed as she turned forward, placing her free hand back on her staff as she once again focused on the wind. "So, he sacrificed you, did he?"

Ronald nodded. "Yes, I do believe he did."

"That's probably for the best. He was more than likely anticipating a punch to the throat, which I gladly would have delivered. But he knows I like you too much for all that. You're gentle with me and everyone else onboard, and in return, I have to be gentle with you," she said with a wink.

He let out an audible sigh. "I guess that makes me pretty lucky." He looked down to the mug and back to her. "Do you want another? Or something to eat? I don't think I've seen you eat a single thing all day."

Mariana shook her head. "I'll eat and drink my fill once we catch that Raider ship. They've destroyed too many villages and killed far too many people. I won't rest easily until their reign of terror is done."

Ronald opened his mouth to speak, but closed it again, thinking over his words carefully. "But you'll need energy if you hope to kick their asses. After all you've been through to hunt them down, don't you want to be strong enough to put an end to them yourself?"

Her eyes darted over to his, lingering for a moment as she

considered his words. Finally, she nodded. "See, Ronald? That's why Veren sent you. He knew that kind heart of yours would be able to talk some sense into me. I would have sent him away with one ball in each hand."

When she saw his eyes widen and heard his sharp intake of breath, she gave him a quick smile and a hard pat on the back. Then she pulled her staff free of its station and its cup of seawater before heading across the deck to find food.

SHE HAD BARELY FINISHED EATING an apple and drinking another pint of ale when the alarms above deck began to sound. She ran up the stairs, staff in hand, and headed back to her station.

"Captain, what is it?" she asked quickly.

He pointed off in the distance. "Smoke. They were here, and from the looks of it, not too long ago."

Mariana's heart sank as she saw the large plumes billowing overhead. It was something she had seen many, many times before, and the scene was always the same. Storm Raiders were cold, ruthless men, and they would stop at nothing to get what they wanted, including ending the lives of innocent men and women, and even young children.

Captain Veren ordered Mariana to steer the ship toward the village. Once they had arrived, everyone armed themselves before making for the smaller boats. Though they didn't want to take weapons, the last thing they wanted was to run into an enemy while unarmed.

Mariana safely delivered everyone to shore, making sure to arrive first so she could inspect the area. While the captain was technically her superior, she was still in charge of everyone else on the ship, just as he was.

She also felt responsible for the innocent lives that had been lost at the hands of the Storm Raiders. A young woman named

Abby, an Arcadian who had settled with her father in Holdgate, had been the biggest reason that the town and all of its storm ships knew about the bastard, Captain Tor, and all the destruction, murder, and pillaging he had done.

Mariana felt partly responsible, having worshipped the ground he walked on, just like everyone else in the town had. In truth, it wasn't her fault at all, but she still felt as though she should have known something was amiss.

Now she dedicated herself to cleaning up the mess that was left, though Abby did a pretty damn good job of it herself. Still, there were straggler ships out and about, always recruiting new people, and she couldn't rest until she found a way to put an end to it.

Screams filled the air, and she looked around to see people scurrying about to save themselves. There weren't many left, as she could see plenty of bodies on the ground.

The screams told her all she needed to know, and she immediately dropped her sword to the ground and held up her hands. She had opted for that instead of the staff, but realized the chunk of wood might have been less threatening. She very slowly took a few steps forward and got down on one knee.

"We're not here to hurt you!" she shouted over the madness.

Some screams halted out of curiosity, but most of the people remaining continued to run around in fear, trying to find a place to hide among the burnt homes.

"Tell me, did their ship look like ours?" she called out.

She heard voices behind her, and she twisted her body just enough to thrust a hand back, signaling for them to stop where they were. She waved her hand downward, and she could see out of her peripheral everyone slowly lowering to their knees.

Turning forward again, she said, "We're hunting a Storm Raider ship. The ship looks like ours, but the sails are different. We only want to help."

Surprisingly, the only person brave enough to step forward

was an elderly woman, her back hunched as she hobbled forward. The clothing she wore was simple, but filthy. It was covered in ash and blood.

"You have magic like theirs," the woman said with obvious hesitation in her voice. Though her body seemed frail, Mariana could tell that she was standing for her people with every ounce of strength she could muster.

Mariana nodded. "We come from the same town. We were all once part of the same fleet. Our goal was to seek out those who would do others harm, but several ships broke off from us and joined the terrible men we hunted. They call themselves 'Storm Raiders'. We are Storm Callers."

The old woman eyed her suspiciously as she took a few shaky steps forward. "You didn't miss 'em by much. They were here only an hour ago, but with the way you folk seem to travel on the surface of the water, I'm guessing that's an eternity, now ain't it?"

A sigh left Mariana as she gave a hesitant nod. "Our magic allows us to call wind to fill our sails, so we can travel faster across the sea. This is the closest we've ever been to that particular ship. Every village we've encountered was destroyed much earlier. While I know it's of little comfort the shortened time lapse between their departure and our arrival means were getting closer."

The woman huffed. "Not close enough, I'm afraid. I'd estimate 90% or more of our village is gone. Men and women run clean through with spears and swords. Young ones burned to death in their beds. You see, we live on the water, too."

The old woman held up her hands, and Mariana saw for the first time the webbing that extended partway up her fingers.

"We live most of our lives in the sea, only coming out to sleep, have babies, and occasionally eat. Most of the time, we just eat fish fresh, without cooking it. Still, we have our homes because our babies and young children don't have access to their magic yet, and us old folk are simply too tired to call on it much anymore."

"I don't mean to be rude, but what point do you have to make?" someone asked from behind Mariana.

She jerked her head around just in time to see Captain Veren punch a man they called Smiley in the arm. "Have some damn respect," the captain snapped.

Satisfied, Mariana turned back around. "Please forgive my rude friend. As you were saying?"

The old woman's eyes lingered on Smiley, and she finally shook her head, once again turning them back to Mariana. "My point…is that while you may not understand us, we are very much the same. You live your life *on* the sea, we live our lives *in* it. Those other men were evil, only using the water as a means to get what they want. I'll trust you, but let it be known that I am an Elder here. I might not look like much to you, and I might not be able to throw a punch, but with a flick of my wrist, I can drown every one of you where you stand. Got it?"

"But if you could do that, why didn't you just kill the Raiders earlier?"

"Dammit, Smiley!" Mariana heard the captain shout behind her, followed by a *thump* and a pain-filled, "*OUCH!*"

"If you want to start with him, it's fine by me," Mariana said, pointing behind her with the jab of thumb.

The old woman sighed and shook her head. "I just might." She turned cold eyes that flashed aquamarine toward Smiley. "As for your question; it's kind of hard to go after the bad guys when you're eighty-five years old and running as fast as your old bones can carry you to round up all the innocent children and hide them. Especially when you get hit in the back of the head and left for dead. How well would you perform magic while uncon-scious? Hmm?"

Mariana couldn't wait for the response to that one. She turned and saw Smiley lower his head in shame, wiping blood from his nose as he mumbled something to the effect of, "I'm sorry."

"Do you have any wounded that need tending to?" Mariana asked.

The woman nodded. "We only had a few healers in the village, and all but one are dead. The last living one here is a young boy who fled south. He had his baby sister with him, so I assume he's heading for our cousin village."

"We don't have any nature magic users, but we certainly know how to stitch up wounds and set broken bones. We'll leave our weapons here and help you save any that can be saved. The rest… well, we'll help you bury them."

The old woman nodded, turning her back as she began to walk away. As promised, Mariana left her weapons, and the rest of the crew did the same as they slowly followed behind.

"You think the boy and little girl are safe?" Mariana asked.

"I certainly hope so. I found one of those Raiders just behind their home. Their parents were slaughtered inside, more than likely protecting the girl. The Raider had been drowned, and I'm afraid it was young Brann who was forced to do it, though I can't be sure. Someone said they saw him make it to the sea with his sister. Honestly, if they'd all stayed in the water, they would still be alive."

"At least they died heroes," Mariana said.

The old woman nodded. "I suppose that's one way to look at it. I overheard one Raider mention a village of Arcadian's, south of the Heights. I assume that's where you'd find them."

"Thank you," Mariana said. "I promise that I will find them, and when I do, they will pay for every life lost. Not only for those here, but in every unfortunate village I've come across during my search."

"I'm glad to hear that, because I have another favor to ask," the old woman replied.

"Anything. What can we do to help?" Mariana asked.

"I mentioned that our cousin village, where young Brann and his sister Sasha are heading, is to the south," she said, and Mariana nodded. "The village is very close to where your Raiders are going to be. When you head down there, while I know it will be difficult, avoid that ship, and check on the village immediately. Tell them what happened. Tell them we sent you there to warn them."

The old woman sighed, stopping and turning to Mariana as she grabbed the Caller's right hand. "They're different than us. They live in the sea, same as we do, but they built their homes inside caves. They made it difficult for anyone to find them. They're stronger than we are; maybe they can help you. Just don't go straight after the Raiders, because I'm telling you now, they have more than twice the men that you do."

Mariana nodded and reached out, squeezing the old woman's hand. "That information helps more than you know. And don't worry about a thing. We'll make sure that they're okay, and I'll personally check on Brann and Sasha."

Without another word, Mariana turned and made her way back to Captain Veren, who was now giving out orders to the men. Mariana took the ones that were the most experienced with wound care, while the rest went with the captain to begin digging graves.

CHAPTER NINE

E smerelda sat on the throne that had once been her husband's, eating fruit from an expensive bowl that had no doubt been pilfered from one of the many homes the bandits had come across in their time living outside of Arcadia.

The tent had been transformed, from a meeting place where the men would gather to discuss barbaric plans while abusing the slaves to a place of entertainment for those who were once their victims.

The tables had turned; she had allowed the women who had suffered so much for so long to deliver their own brand of justice. Whatever they saw fit was fine by her.

As the new queen sat on her usurped throne, she watched the men walk around in only loincloths to hide themselves as they danced, served wine, fed the women grapes, and cut up pieces of fruit.

She smiled as a tall man with broad shoulders approached her —defiant, though his eyes were downcast. Just by looking at him, she could tell exactly how much he hated her.

But he followed her every command.

"Hello, Charles," she said in a seductive voice. "And why have you approached me?"

His brows furrowed, his fists slightly clenching at his sides. "*Forgive me* for interrupting," he said with utter disdain, "but you have kept us here like dogs—"

"Oh," she said, feigning a concerned expression as she sat forward. "I *do* hope they're *grateful* dogs. After all, when the dog bites the hand of his master… Well, I believe the new ancients had a saying about that. Don't you?"

Esmerelda watched as two women approached from behind, swords drawn and pointed directly at his back. They watched him carefully as the situation unfolded. He had once been a highly ranked guard in Adrien's army, which had given him incredible senses. His eyes and stiffening posture told her that he knew they were there.

The man smiled through gritted teeth, giving a curt nod. "We are all—*so*—very grateful, Esmerelda," he said pointedly. "However, the men *do* feel our talents are being unused. Some of them feel we're wasting precious time that we could be using to advance."

She smiled. "Is that so? And by '*them*', do you mean *you*?"

His eyes met hers then, icy blue irises boring into her. "I do. I get that you're trying to have your fun, trying to get back something you feel was taken from you. But at the risk of being run through with those blades behind me, you're acting like a child that's been given a brand new toy."

Her eyes widened slightly as a small smile spread across her face. "'Child'? My, those are awfully brave words coming from a man in a loincloth, dancing for his keepers' entertainment to save his own skin."

A dark smile crossed his lips in return. "I'm only biding my time until one of two things happen: you either get off your ass and use the talent that's right in front of you, or we kill you and take back what's rightfully ours."

Standing, Esmerelda took a quick step forward and thrust out her hand to wrap around his throat, pulling him down to her and pressing her lips against his. There was a fierceness in the action, a need, and it obviously took him by surprise.

But it ended as quickly as it began.

Taking a step back, Esmerelda said, "Oh, Charles. I believe that you and I have a *very* different opinion on what is rightfully yours."

Taking another step back, she smiled again as his eyes went wide and his jaw fell slack. Painful, gasping breaths gurgled from his throat. With another shove, the blades pierced through to the front of his body.

In unison, the women pulled back, their swords making a slick sound as they slid out, causing his body to fall to the ground. There were several gasps from men in the tent who had taken notice, but others were smart enough to keep their eyes down and not say a word.

Placing her hands on her hips, Esmerelda looked down, pursing her lips for a moment. "But you *do* make a very good point."

She looked around the tent, taking in the sight of her warrior women getting their varying ideas of revenge on the men who were now their slaves. Charles wasn't wrong. There was a lot of muscle being wasted.

Well, not wasted, she thought with humor. *But certainly not used to its full potential.*

Holding up her hands, she watched as her warriors began quieting the men that had begun to brave whispers. Soon everyone in the room was silent, and all eyes were on her.

"I'm hurt. Really. You still don't understand the wrongs you have made here in the past? I had hoped that you would learn some humility, knowing what it felt like to be treated as less than human. Somehow, though, that lesson has been lost."

She stared out at the crowd, allowing her words to sink in. "It seems that Charles here felt we were not making good use of you.

From what I hear—" she smiled "—we've been making *very* good use of you. But there might be some truth to what he said. Show of hands, how many of you men feel the same way he did?"

There were several moments of hesitation as the men looked at one another, trying to decide if it was a trap.

"I'm asking! No worries here. At this moment, this is a kill-free zone. So, I will ask you only once more. Who here feels their talents are being wasted?"

Several hands slowly lifted. When no one was gutted where they stood, several more lifted. Soon, every man under the tent had a hand in the air.

Esmerelda smiled. "Thank you for your honesty. Now I'm going to be honest with you. You were given the option before, but it seems many of you have been hesitant to actually show enthusiasm for my rule. So, I'm going to give you an opportunity I had previously decided I wouldn't. But make no mistake… This is the very last time this opportunity will arise."

She watched as arms lowered and the men once again looked at one another with confusion, trying to decipher her meaning.

Instead of allowing them to wonder any longer, she continued. "You were given the choice to follow me or die. You chose to follow, but you haven't shown any excitement for doing so. Now is your last chance. Show of hands. Who among you would follow me into war?"

Hands immediately shot up, several voices cheering out while others hesitantly whispered with their neighbors.

She smiled. "See? Was that so hard? As you all know, my late husband always made promises to raid the Heights. He wanted to take Craigston as well as the Temple. Unfortunately for all of you, my husband was weak. I, however, am not. Who among you will follow me into the mountains? Who among you will fight not only *for* me, but *alongside* me?"

Shocking even her, the excitement in the room blossomed. Men began to shout and cheer for her. Others followed suit, but she could tell it was forced. It was easy to tell who was motivated by greed and who was motivated by power—or fear. Anyone cheering for her obviously cared more about money and possessions; the rest would fight for her, but would secretly be planning her downfall.

Ignoring the latter group for the time being, she raised her arms out to her side and smiled. "Then let this be the dawn of a new day. Men, you will train with the women in hand-to-hand combat, as well as in magitech weaponry. And don't get any ideas —only a few of you will be chosen, and those that are will be heavily guarded by their mistresses. So be on your best behavior. Impress me, and you will not regret it."

With the wave of a hand, she dismissed everyone, then motioned for her two personal guards to come forward.

"No more than one man to a group of four to five women. While we have a lot of skills they aren't aware of, they still have years of combat training on us, and a hundred pounds of muscle. They can move incredibly fast, so let's not give them the chance to turn," Esmerelda said.

"How will we know who to choose?" Jill asked.

"As I was making my speech, I could tell who was genuinely excited about the trip, and who only pretended to be in order to save his own skin. Interview them. You'll know who is who. They aren't terribly bright, which was why Adrien chose them—as well as my husband. They'll make it obvious."

The women gave a quick nod before turning to walk away. Esmerelda stepped forward, stopping them for a moment. "Before you go, make sure everyone knows we will be heading out in thirty-six hours. At their skill level, it won't take long for us to learn what we must in order to proceed, and I need to demonstrate my power quickly, before there is a mutiny."

Dark smiles crossed the women's faces as excitement took hold of them. They nodded before turning away and heading out of the tent to complete their orders.

CHAPTER TEN

By the time Arryn and her group arrived in Craigston, the sun had nearly set. High in the mountains, the sky was grey, and there was a distinct chill in the air that hadn't been present in the valley.

"It's about ta snow," Samuel said with a smile on his face. "It's good ta be home."

Arryn smiled. "I bet it is. We should definitely make a plan before getting all the way into town. Are we stopping at Ophelia's, or going straight to your house?"

Samuel laughed. "We get a keg an' then head back ta my house, lass. Did ye really need ta ask that?"

"Yeah, *lass*, did you really need to ask?" Cathillian asked as he rode up beside Arryn.

Arryn rolled her eyes and shook her head, as she usually did when Cathillian was being slightly ridiculous. "You know, I—"

"Hold on, there, lass." Samuel brought his horse forward, moving past Arryn and Cathillian as he studied the area.

When Arryn sensed his apprehension, she immediately became more serious. Looking around, she searched for what Samuel might be seeing or hearing. From what she could tell, there was more buzzing in the streets than usual. More than that, the rearick walking around seem to be very sober.

"Boy, that *is* something to worry about. Rearick running around sober?" Cathillian said.

Arryn shot him a look, but it wasn't quite as stern as she had meant for it to be, considering she had been thinking the same thing.

"Shut yer trap, little boy," Samuel said.

Cathillian opened his mouth to fake his offense as he usually did, but Samuel was quick to interrupt him. He no doubt knew Cathillian was about to make some smartass comment, even without looking at him. "They're sober 'cause they're headin' ta the medical buildin'."

Snow grumbled a bit, and Arryn reached through the bond.

"Snow says she smells blood," Arryn said. "But it isn't fresh. Not all of it, anyway."

Samuel pointed his horse toward the medical building, and Arryn was quick to follow. When they reached their destination, Snow lowered herself to the ground, and Arryn dismounted, giving her a quick scratch before she went to catch up with Samuel.

"Excuse me," Arryn said to one of the rearick passing through. "What happened here?"

A rearick woman who was a few inches shorter than Samuel, but looked twice as mean, stopped hard. She turned and looked at Arryn, her brows furrowing as she moved her eyes over the druid's entire length, sizing her up. She almost seemed offended.

"Remnant. Not that you'd care, *Arcadian*." The woman almost spat the words.

"Ethel, ye right twat," Samuel said. "There ain't no need ta be such a beast. She's tryin' ta help."

Ethel scoffed. "Is that so, ye ol' bastard? So, ye got a thing fer outsiders, do ye? Ye like living with 'em, do ye? Well, those men an' women in there got hurt fightin' off the remnant. Injured doin' what they were meant ta do—protectin' their own. Where were *you*?"

Ignoring almost everything the woman had said, Arryn only responded to the part that meant anything to her. After all, rearick insulted each other regularly; if a rearick didn't insult someone at least once in a conversation, it was pretty certain he or she didn't like the person. "Remnant have been coming out this way?"

The woman turned cold eyes toward Arryn. "A little over a week ago. But we sent the ones we didn't kill running like the little bitches they are."

"I don't doubt that for a second," Arryn said. "Rearick are some of the strongest fighters I've ever seen. That doesn't mean they have to lay there in pain."

The woman eyed her suspiciously, then turned her eyes to the side a little, where Arryn could feel Cathillian's presence. "Maybe yer not Arcadians, after all, but ye still ain't—"

Samuel groaned loudly as he stepped forward and clapped his hand down on the woman's shoulder. "Yes, she is. She an' that tall, pretty, girly boy over there—"

"Hey!" Cathillian interjected, but Samuel continued as if he hadn't heard him.

"—are gonna go in there an' heal whatever injuries they can. We rearick have our pride, and I get that. I ain't lost mine. But I've come ta know there are some things more important than pride—like the ability ta care fer one's family. How can those people get back in the mines and earn coin if they're disabled fer the rest o' their damned lives? How important is pride then?"

Ethel grumbled to herself before shaking her head and turning toward the entrance of the building. Without saying a word, she nodded in the direction of the door, signaling for them to follow.

Arryn smiled at Samuel, amused by watching him argue on her behalf. "Thanks for volunteering me."

He shot her an incredulous look. "Hush. We both know ye were gonna fight yer way in there, one way 'r another."

She smiled again. "You know me too well."

The building was not quite as full as she had expected. There were only about ten people stuck in beds, but they had terrible wounds. A few of them had been run through with a weapon of some kind, a couple were missing limbs, and there were even a couple in a coma.

Arryn and Cathillian saw to them first, healing what had been severe head traumas. As they woke, each patient became very emotional, crying as they reached out for Arryn and Cathillian.

Though Arryn found that reaction to be very surprising—coming from a rearick—she was less surprised by the rearick standing around turning their backs on the spectacle. They weren't a very emotional bunch. Weakness was weakness, though there were exceptions. Those standing around found it to be more respectful to turn their backs and give the person space than to witness their vulnerability.

Arryn couldn't do anything about the few with severed limbs, but she was able to heal the wounds left behind so they could get on with their lives. It had taken a little coaxing, but with Samuel's help, there wasn't too much protesting about magic use.

"Are you ready for that drink, yet?" Samuel asked as Arryn approached after healing her last patient. "Because I sure am."

She smiled. "Oh, are you? How many people did you heal today?"

Samuel looked taken aback as he quickly leaned forward. "Shh! Shut yer mouth, lass!" he whispered forcefully. "If the others knew about... Well, ye know." He lowered his voice even further. "About me magic..."

Arryn nodded. "Yeah, yeah. I know. Ye'd get yer arse kicked," she said, copying his accent over the last sentence.

He leaned back and smiled. "Hey. Yer gettin' pretty good at that."

"Are the two of you done making out now? Because I'd love to get a drink," Bast said from just outside the door. They had waited with Corrine and the animals to keep out of the way. "I wanna get drunk. Pass out. And go hunt down some assholes. Sounds like fun, yeah?"

"I'm not sure." Arryn looked down at Samuel. "Are we done making out?"

He looked at her with a shocked expression. "Get outta here before I kick ye out. What's the matter with ye girls? Yer supposed ta be frilly—'r some shit like that."

"I do believe his little face is turning red," Bast said, pointing at Samuel. "Does that mean it's about to explode?"

The rearick nearly opened his mouth to protest, but Arryn clapped him on the back. "Relax, lad. You stay here and cool off. Send Cathillian out when he's done flirting with the patients. Bast and I are going to the bar so we can pass out, wake up, and hunt down some assholes first thing in the morning."

"Ye can start with that arsehole right there," Ethel said casually with a nod toward Samuel in passing.

The girls laughed loudly as they made their way out of the medical building. Just as Arryn stepped out the door, she poked her head back in, giving Samuel a genuine smile and a wink.

The rearick smiled in response before shooing her out the door with his hands.

When Arryn and Bast got back to Cleo and Corrine, they found them straddling a log, and Cleo playing with Corrine's braids while the little girl petted the rabbit. Snow and Dante were cuddled up together on the ground, and the horses stood nearby.

"Damn. You guys finally finished making out in there?" Cleo asked.

Arryn looked at her incredulously before turning to Bast and shaking her head. "Yep. Twins." Turning back to Cleo and Corrine, she said, "We're going to the bar to grab a keg of mystic's brew; it'll help us relax and get some sleep. Tomorrow is a big day. We have to trek down the other side of the mountain."

"Sounds good to me," Cleo said. "My ass is killing me from being on that damn horse all day, though. I'll walk. You lead the way."

The friendly white rabbit jumped out of Corrine's lap and onto the ground, and Arryn noticed a bit of green fur around his little feet. She laughed and knelt to the ground.

"Mr. Snoogletoosh, your feet are stained from the grass, I think."

The rabbit ran into Arryn's arms, and she lifted him, inspecting his feet. Around the bottom, they were dark green—almost the color of the leaves in the trees in midsummer—but just on top and around the lower part of his legs, they were a lighter green.

"Maybe he should stay off the grass for a while. His poor snowy white fur is getting all stained from the journey," Arryn said with a smile. She put him down on the ground, and he ran back to Corrine.

The little girl smiled as she picked him up. "Well, he rode most of the way in my lap on Dante, but he can definitely stay with me even more. I don't mind."

Arryn smiled and stood, and Snow and Dante followed suit as they made their way to Ophelia's.

"Why is it that the women are heading to get the booze, while the guys stand around and chat?" Cleo asked.

There was a laugh from a passing rearick woman. "Welcome ta Craigston, lassies. We haven't a feckin' clue, either."

tree, quickly followed by a child screaming as he hit the ground.

Before she even had time to react, she felt a burst of power come from Corrine, and vines shot down from all over the massive tree, picking every child up and carrying them high into the branches. She was protecting them.

Snow let loose a roar meant to send Arryn running. She could feel the tiger calling her through the bond. Dante and Snow leapt from the branches in the tree, their heads lowered as they growled ominously at something Arryn couldn't see. Dante was even larger that morning, having grown several inches overnight, from the looks of it.

Arryn flung the door open, turning toward the inside. "EVERYBODY UP NOW! *MOVE, MOVE, MOVE!*" she screamed out.

She turned and ran—half-naked and with no shoes—into the cold. She could hear the whistling of dozens of arrows shooting through the air, and her adrenaline spiked.

Arryn ran harder beneath the tree, her eyes turning black as she allowed her magic to wrap around her. Her magic pulsed, transporting her from where she ran to directly under the tree. Without hesitation or even taking a breath, Arryn thrust her hands outward, causing a magical shield to burst forth.

It was the size of a large wall, and was tall enough to shield the familiars, Arryn, Corrine, and all the children in the tree. The magic was a translucent pink, so Arryn was able to see every arrow strike as the shield deflected them.

"Snow!" Arryn called out as women and men ran through the trees and into the opening.

Snow and Dante darted off in opposite directions, running around the shield to attack the crowd at opposite sides. Echo screeched overhead, having returned sometime in the night. She dove down, forcing several people to the ground as the tigers pounced on them.

"Corrine, get into the tree with the other children," Arryn said. When Corrine started to protest, Arryn interrupted. "They have *no* magic. None. If something happens, they *will* die. You're the best healer we have. Get up there."

A look of determination came across Corrine's face as a vine appeared and lifted her up into the branches. Once she was safe and out of the way, Arryn dropped the shield and ran forward.

Fuck me, she thought, knowing she had no weapons.

A man came at her with a sword, swinging it with one hand. She moved to the side, but the blade caught her thigh as she pulled it back too late. Only letting out a single grunt of pain, she stepped into him and wrapped one arm around the one that held the sword. With his free hand, he grabbed a fist of her hair, and she countered with a knee to the groin.

He cried out, and she repeated the move, loosening his grip enough that she was able to stand upright again. She flexed her arm as tight as she could and jerked, breaking his elbow and causing him to drop the sword.

As he fell back, she dropped to the ground, grabbed the weapon, and turned just in time to run him through with it.

"Thanks. I needed one of these," she said as she shoved harder and then twisted before pulling it free.

Warmth filled her leg, and she looked down to see the wound knitting itself back together. Her eyes darted up to see neon green orbs glowing in the shadows of the leaves.

"Higher in the tree than that," she said, smiling. "And thank you. Don't waste your magic on the small stuff. I'll be fine."

She looked forward to see over a dozen men and women now coming for her. Snow and Dante were busy with others, farther back.

"Then again..." she said, lifting her sword.

Two shadows passed above only a second before the ground quaked beneath her. The twins landed several feet ahead, directly between Arryn and the oncoming mob.

The resulting blast of power that moved through the ground was enough to almost knock Arryn off balance. She heard screams from high in the tree as a few children tumbled, but Corrine was fast, and snatched them back up with vines.

More screams erupted from just ahead, and she looked to see Bast and Cleo punching and kicking opponents.

A shift in the air behind her caught her attention, and she turned just in time to dodge a knife to the face. She heard a yelp from behind her and turned to see an angry Cleo with raging blue eyes, pulling a knife from her thigh.

Looking back to the man who had thrown it, Arryn said, "Uhh… You should probably run. You're not going to like what happens next."

His eyes only widened as the knife whizzed back past Arryn's head, and struck him directly in the face. While the blade entered like it would have into warm butter, the hilt caved in the entire front half of his skull. With the amount of power the angry Kemetian had called upon, Arryn was surprised his head hadn't exploded.

"I *really* need to never piss Cleo off," Arryn said to herself.

Then she waved her hand, and a knife in the man's belt quickly levitated to Arryn. She tossed it in the air once, catching the tip of the blade in her hand, before throwing it hard at the next person coming at her. It stuck in the woman's chest, and Arryn ran for the next.

"ARRYN'S GOING to fucking kill us before the enemy does," Cathillian said, rushing around the cabin looking for his shirt, boots, and sword. "Where the *fuck* did I put everything? Oh, Bitch and Bastard, she's going to kill me. I would have been dressed, if you didn't keep it so blasted hot in here!"

"I think yer more scared o' that girl than ye are the enemies outside. And don't pick on me heating. Kept all yer arses warm, didn't it?" Samuel said, also running around and searching for items. "Where's me bastard axe!"

"I *am* scared of her!" Cathillian nearly shouted. "We should have been out there by now! I can't find my shirt or my boots. I'm never letting you talk me into drinking that shit again."

There was a pause as Samuel looked outside. "Uh, lad," he said, a bit of warning in his voice. "She's gonna kill us both. She's out there damn near naked. The twins may as well be naked, too, and we're in here tryna find clothes and weapons. Ain't one of 'em got a sword or knife, and they're takin' 'em down right and left."

The color drained from Cathillian's face as the two men looked at one another. "Maybe we should just go."

Samuel nodded. "I think that's safer than tryna find 'r weapons while they do all the work."

"At this point, I'd rather go blindfolded and naked than to answer to any of them after this," Cathillian said while quickly heading for the door.

"Same, lad. You didn't just see what Cleo did ta some poor arsehole out there. His head damn near came clean off."

Cathillian caught something in his peripheral. He looked up and saw Samuel's axe stuck in the log ceiling, almost six feet over his head.

Memories slowly started to come back, and he remembered the rearick giving him a hard time. In return, Cathillian had taken the axe and heaved it up over his head, burying it in the ceiling.

"I found the axe," Cathillian said.

Samuel looked up. "Hmmph. Yeah, now I remember what ye did ta me baby, ye tall bastard."

Cathillian ran at the wall, jumping up and planting a foot on it before pushing off, giving him the vertical leap needed to grab the handle and pull it free. He landed gracefully with barely any sound at all and handed it back to the rearick.

"There. Now, let's get out there before we get skewered," Cathillian said.

Both men ran outside, Cathillian only barely allowing himself a moment to adjust to the drastic temperature change. It hit him hard as he sucked in a cold breath. He had on his brown leather pants, but wore no weapons, boots, or shirt.

As he ran off the large wooden deck, he almost slipped on a bit of snow along the edge, but he managed to keep his footing as he ran as hard as he could toward the group descending upon Arryn.

Cathillian leapt into the air, flipping over once before planting his feet firmly in the chest of an approaching man. They both hit the ground hard, but Cathillian was quick to roll over and whip his hand upward. A tree root burst from the ground, piercing through his foe's chest and killing him.

The druid quickly stood, stole the dead man's sword, and narrowly deflected a strike from a woman that had come for him.

"So nice of you to finally join us," Arryn said with a grunt as she ran the woman through with her own pilfered sword. "You look positively beautiful this morning. Must've been all that beauty sleep you got."

"Actually, I do feel quite rested, thank you. Notice that I'm out here half-naked, too," he said.

She looked at him incredulously. "Was that before or after you took forever looking for the shit you left in my room when I kicked you out for snoring?"

He looked guilty for a moment before smiling and twisting his hand. A snow-covered vine burst from the ground and wrapped around the neck of a man that had come up behind Arryn. With a flick of his wrist, Cathillian broke the man's neck and cast him aside.

Arryn didn't flinch as she stared Cathillian down.

"I'm sorry!" he said. "I forgot I left it in there. Shit, I thought I slept on the couch all night. I don't even remember being in your room."

Arryn rolled her eyes and shook her head. "Good to know. You're not drinking the hard shit with Samuel anymore. I thought we learned our lesson the last time when I got shit-faced with him." She pointed behind Cathillian.

"Is this our first fight?" Cathillian asked, turning to clash swords with two men who had snuck up from behind.

Crackling sounds whizzed past either side of his head, and the men in front of him burst into flames. He turned his head to see Arryn's eyes fading from black to their normal brown.

"Don't make this weird. You're making it weird."

She took off in the opposite direction, dropping the sword she held for a bow and quiver she found on the ground.

"She's the most confusing woman I've ever met," Cathillian said to himself. "But that's probably why I love her."

He turned again and headed into the crowd the large tigers were taking on, knowing Arryn would be fine on her own.

CHAPTER TWELVE

Arryn was running out of energy, and she didn't want to waste any more than necessary on magic. She ran toward the house with the bow and quiver that she'd picked up from the ground. She heard another loud screech from Echo as the large raptor bird dove after someone running away to knock them to the ground.

The attacking group was well-prepared; whatever they wanted, whatever they were after, they had come heavily armed. The quiver was stuffed to the max, overflowing.

The fact caught Arryn off guard, and she suddenly believed they might not be dealing with a well-trained group—even if that group was well-armed and seemingly prepared.

Overstuffing the quiver would only slow the user down when pulling arrows from it; they would either pull out too many, or the arrows would become stuck on their way out. She would have to correct this before it would be of use to her.

Once Arryn was safely on the roof, she dumped some arrows out between her bare feet, where she could still reach them if needed. Then she slung the quiver over her shoulder, pulled an arrow free, nocked it, and aimed.

It only took but a second to pick out an enemy approaching the large tree where the children were located. The man looked up, but as soon as he took the first step to start his climb, Arryn put an arrow in his spine, dropping him instantly.

Next, she looked over to Bast and Cleo. They still fought hard, but she could tell they were using no more than regular strength. Their magic required a *lot* of energy, and they couldn't use it for long. Not in battle, anyway.

She nocked another arrow and aimed. Again. And again. Within only a few seconds, Arryn took out several of their opponents, thinning the crowd for them.

Off to the north, Arryn saw a woman fleeing while frantically looking back over her shoulder to make sure no one was following. Arryn's eyes narrowed as she nocked another arrow. She pulled back and loosed it, striking the woman in the back of the leg. She tumbled to the ground, only the faintest cry reaching Arryn's ears across the distance.

Arryn's eyes flashed green as she reached through the bond to Dante.

Out of her periphery, she saw the overgrown tiger cub rushing to the location she'd shown him. She heard the woman scream as Dante lowered and roared at her to intimidate her into submission.

It didn't take much. The woman simply curled into a ball, seemingly awaiting the worst.

Keep her there, Arryn told Dante.

The tiger plopped down on his backside while still keeping a tall, regal posture, watching his captive carefully. Arryn smiled as she jumped from the roof, vines lifting to wrap around her and safely lower her to the ground.

The fight was winding down, and any attackers who hadn't been killed had fled.

Arryn made her way over to the tree and looked up, Echo was

just overhead and flying to that very tree. "Corrine. Is everyone okay up there?"

The girl flipped around a branch and dropped to the ground, landing gracefully on her bare feet. "All okay. I even got to throw in a few heals."

Arryn smiled. "Glad to hear it, and I'm glad you got to feel useful. As great of a healer as you are now, you will be an even better fighter when you get older."

Corrine smiled and stepped forward, wrapping her arms around Arryn and hugging her tight. "I think I'd do okay even now. You're just a little too overprotective."

"Honestly, I'm sure you *would* do okay. But who in their right mind would allow an eight-year-old to fight if there was no true need for it? I know you've had to do it before, and I'm sure you'll have to do it again, but I'm not just going to throw you into the mix unless you absolutely have to be there."

With a sigh, Corrine nodded. "I understand."

"How about you get all of those kids down and take Snow and the twins with you to escort them back to town?" Arryn said, twisting one of Corrine's braids in her fingers.

The little girl's eyes flashed neon green as she took a step back and lifted her hands. She watched the tree as vines began to weave through the branches and wrap around the kids before lowering them to the ground.

Corrine reassured them that they were safe as she walked them over to Bast and Cleo.

Arryn turned in Dante's direction, but Samuel and Cathillian stepped in her way, smiles on their faces, and bodies covered in blood and dirt.

"Yer not angry, right?" Samuel asked. "Yer not gonna stake us in our sleep?"

Arryn smiled. "Oh, I don't need you to be asleep to do that."

Cathillian and Samuel looked at one another with obvious worry, and Arryn laughed.

"Relax. I've got bigger things on my mind than punishing the two of you for being late to the party. Everything turned out okay, and none of us died, so we'll talk about that later. Right now, Dante is waiting for me. He has one of our attackers subdued with an arrow in her thigh."

With that, she gave a chipper smile and turned to walk away.

Now that the adrenaline was gone, Arryn could feel the chill in the air really biting her skin. Stubborn as she was, she couldn't bring herself to show that she was uncomfortable. She could tell Cathillian was in the same boat; both of them too stubborn to admit they needed to go find clothes.

When she arrived, Dante was once again standing on all fours, his lips pulled back in a terrifying snarl. It looked as though his captive had tried to run at least once. The arrow in her leg had been broken off but not removed.

"Good morning, sweet cheeks," Arryn said as she walked over to the woman on the ground.

"Fuck off," the woman said flatly, scooting back to a more comfortable position.

"I'm good, but thank you for the offer." Arryn crouched down, smiling as she tilted her head to the side. "We can do this the easy way, where you answer my questions, or we can do this the hard way. Just as an FYI, there are many hard ways, and none of them are pleasant."

"Fuck off," the woman said again. "I'm not telling you anything."

"Okay, then. Hard way, it is." Arryn stood and waved a hand in her direction. "Dante."

Dante growled as he stepped forward and opened his jaws, preparing to bite down on her calf.

"Wh-wh-whoa!" the woman protested, scooting back further. "Wait a minute. Aren't you supposed to be the good guys? Aren't you supposed to give me a few chances, or some shit?"

Arryn quirked her brow. "I'm sorry. Did you mistake me for

the forgiving type? If you accidentally bump into me. Forgiven. If you have a bad day and say something that shouldn't be said. Forgiven. When you bring weapons and threaten the lives of dozens of children... There are *no* second chances. The only choice you will be given is just how gently you want to die."

The woman stared at Arryn fearfully. "What are my options?"

"First: you can answer my questions willingly, and I will end you quickly," Arryn offered.

The woman on the ground shook her head. "Next. That doesn't give me enough opportunity to slip away."

Arryn sighed, rubbing the bridge of her nose. "Yeah, I don't think you'll have much opportunity in any case. Then we go with option number two. We pay a visit to my dear friends at the Temple"

She shook her head again. "No. You may as well kill me now. I'm not very good with mental magic, but I know how to create a mental block. You won't get anywhere with me."

Arryn shrugged. "A second ago, you wanted an opportunity to slip away. Now you're saying to kill you. Interesting. In any case, you're absolutely right. I can't." She nodded toward the Temple. "But they will. In fact, I know just the badass old lady to take you to."

The woman on the ground laughed. "Go right on ahead. Esmerelda won't allow me to be taken hostage. My friends will come for me. That's if I don't escape first." She gave a smug grin, and Arryn gave one of her own.

With the flick of her wrist, thorny vines sprouted from the tree line and wrapped around her captive's wrists, securing them to her waist before wrapping around each ankle and lashing them together.

"Escape that," Arryn said before another vine wrapped around the woman's waist and picked her up. "Cathillian, do you mind?"

Cathillian smiled and nodded, stepping forward as his jade

eyes flashed greener. As they walked, new vines sprouted every so often, carrying their hostage toward the house.

"I believe I have somethin' we can tie 'er to. We can't let 'er ride on the animals, 'r those thorns'll stick 'em. Instead, Snow or Dante can drag 'er along behind. That ought ta be a bumpy enough ride ta teach her a lesson 'r two," Samuel said.

"Good. If were going higher into the mountains, though, I'll need some damn clothes—so will this blonde bastard," Arryn said.

"Hey, I already vowed never to get that drunk again. Well, at least not while we aren't safe within the Dark Forest. Wasn't one of my finer ideas," Cathillian said.

"Somehow, I doubt you have very many fine ideas," the captive said. "Not that I can complain about the view."

"At least someone around here appreciates me," Cathillian said.

Arryn laughed. "I'm sure she does. Take her back to your mom. Let's see how she likes your new friend. I'm sure they'll be best friends."

Samuel scoffed. "Lad, I'd quit crackin' jokes, if I were you. We're on thin ice as it is. Flirtin' with the hostage ain't gettin' you nothin' but buried deeper. Besides, we all know Elysia would eat that girl for breakfast if she stepped foot in the Dark Forest."

"You're druids? I've never seen one. Wait... Druids eat people?" the captive asked with obvious worry in her voice.

Arryn turned and smiled, her eyes flashing green. "We sure do. And I'm getting *super* hungry. Must've been all that fighting."

The woman's eyes widened as she quickly shut her mouth and faced away from Arryn.

Once Bast, Cleo, and Corrine came back from returning the children to their homes, the party made their way further up the mountain, heading toward the Temple.

As promised, Samuel fashioned a gurney of sorts for the

hostage and strapped it to Snow's back. Cathillian's familiar flew circles above as she slowly followed the group.

Despite the circumstances, Arryn was actually excited to return to the Temple. She hadn't visited since the mystics helped her create a mental block to defend against Scarlett, while she was searching for a way to liberate Arcadia.

She had learned a few other tricks while at the Temple, but she hadn't exactly been practicing them. Telepathy seemed like an invasion of privacy to her, but the ability to read people and sense them like a mystic could—well, that could come in handy.

As they arrived at the Temple doors, they were met with the usual guards.

"Welcome, druids," one of the guards said. "What brings you to the Temple?"

Arryn gestured behind her, to the woman strapped to a gurney. "This woman was one of many who attacked my rearick friend on his property. Three of our party went into town to escort children back home, where they discovered there had been an attack on Craigston directly. All of those intruders were killed quickly by the rearick. It seems the majority attacked us. I would assume they were heading toward you, but I can't be sure. I brought our little friend here for an interrogation."

Arryn felt the familiar buzz in her mind, letting her know someone was trying to look inside of it. She immediately released the mental block to allow them full access.

As they looked through her memories from the past twenty-four hours, she could see snippets of what they pulled forward. Once they were finished, their eyes faded back to their normal color.

"Margit will want to see you right away. Master Julianne has gone back to Tahn on official business."

Arryn nodded. As the guards turned to open the doors, She turned to Cathillian. "*Damn.* I'm always missing her; I don't think I'm ever going to get a chance to meet her."

The guard she had been speaking to smiled as he motioned inside. "She would like to meet you, as well. She has heard a great deal about you, and Margit has spoken very highly of you."

Echo landed on a ledge high on the Temple as Snow and Dante followed Arryn inside.

"Good to know. And here I thought the old woman thought I was a scatterbrain."

An elderly woman rounded the corner, one of her eyebrows raised, and her arms crossed. "Who said I don't?"

Arryn smiled. "Margit! So happy to see you. You're like a vision of myself from the future: old and snarky as hell, but a badass, so nobody calls me out on my bullshit."

The old mystic shook her head. "Scatterbrain, indeed. Get inside. I know you must be hungry after your journey. Leave your friend with our guards; I can assure you, if she tries to escape as she *thinks* she can, they will have her convinced she's a dog, and doing tricks in the courtyard for treats faster than you can say 'Bethany Anne.'"

Arryn laughed. "Maybe we can make that happen before we leave, anyway. Sounds like a good time."

Margit turned and motioned for them to follow behind. "Zoe will be so happy to see you. Goddess help me when you're together."

CHAPTER THIRTEEN

It had been a few days since Brann had arrived at the southern village on the Farriage Coast. His Daoine cousins had been excited to see him, but that excitement quickly faded when they heard the fate of his home.

His parents were dead, but he had managed to save his sister; it was the best he could do in the situation he had been given, and he was proud of himself for that.

Finn and his pod had stayed close to Brann, never wandering too far. Brann imagined it was worry keeping them there.

While it had been days since Brann had seen the storm ship, his gut told him they weren't far away.

The day he arrived, everyone had stayed inside the cave as he told them about the horrors he had seen. He and the Elders then spoke at great length about what happened and formulated a plan, should the Raiders return.

"Is that Finn?" one of his younger cousins, Zhaun, asked.

Brann looked out and saw a smaller dolphin breaching, its tail scarred but strong. He nodded. "Sure is. He's my best friend in the water."

The little boy almost sparkled. He had only recently been

cleared by the Elders to swim alone. His magic was finally strong enough to propel him quickly through any crashing waves that may come on.

"And is it true you can talk to him?" he asked.

Brann smiled. His gift was rare. He was only one of a very few who could communicate with marine mammals, and even then, it was spotty. "Kind of. We can't talk to one another in complete sentences or anything, but I can feel when he feels scared, and he can do the same for me. We communicate through emotions mostly, but I can somehow understand some of the sounds he makes, and he can understand some of my words."

"I wanna be able to do that, too!" young Zhaun said.

"I wish I could teach you, but I honestly wouldn't have a clue how. It just kind of happened. I think it was because I healed him when he was just a baby."

Thunder cracked in the distance, and a cold chill ran down Brann's spine. He looked up to see the beautiful blue sky beginning to darken. He heard splashing off to the left and turned to see the pod of dolphins quickly heading in another direction.

Finn swam up from under Brann, catching him off guard and startling him. The dolphin then grabbed Brann's arm in his mouth and began pulling.

"What is it? What's happening?" Zhaun asked.

Another roll of thunder boomed out, and the shadows of clouds began to fall over them. Brann turned to Zhaun, worry clearly written on his face. "Swim. Fast. Get back to the cave and tell everyone on your way to do the same."

Zhaun didn't stick around to ask more questions. He simply turned and swam northwest, back to their underwater cave.

Brann frantically looked around, searching for the Elders. Most were in charge of watching over the younger children inside the cave and on land, but the most capable of them were always in the water, watching over the family and teaching the children.

He rushed over to the first group he saw. They were treading water and looking at the sky in confusion.

"Get to the cave! It's the storm ship!" he told them.

Panic spread across their faces as they turned, ducked under the surface of the water, and swam for the cave. Looking northeast, he saw the first outline of the ship come into view. It was miles away, but he knew all too well just how fast it was able to move.

Movement caught his attention, and he turned to see Finn once again staring at him, his mother not far away. Brann pushed all the emotion he could toward the mammal as he pointedly looked to his scattered family and back to Finn. *"Help me."*

There seemed to be a moment of confusion, but when Brann dove under the water, his eyes glowing aqua as he powered through, Finn darted off in another direction.

"Lorelei!" Brann called out, just after bringing his head above water.

The Elder turned to him, her smile fading as she registered his worry. He pointed off in the distance, and Lorelei turned to see the ship.

"Storm ship!" Lorelei shouted, her voice carrying farther than Brann's would have been capable of.

Elders all over began to call out, warning everyone to swim for the cave. The plan was for all the young children to go first, accompanied by the older children. The Elders would then hold back and make sure no stragglers were left behind before going inside.

No one was to swim on the surface, though almost no one did that anyway, when swimming for speed. To travel under the water was much faster than fighting the currents on the surface.

In only the short few minutes that Brann had taken to warn everyone, and watch as they fled to safety, the ship had closed the distance enough to almost double in size. While they were certainly large enough for him to see, he doubted they could see him or anyone else. They were moving fast, but because of his quick response, the risk of them being found was slim.

"Brann!" Lorelei shouted. "Inside!"

Thunder cracked again, lightning webbing across the sky as Brann once again dove under the surface. As he swam toward the large, mountainous cliff that housed the entrance to their hideaway, he passed Finn and his mother. They were leaving the mouth of the cave and heading south, in the direction of their fleeing pod.

A feeling of relief washed over him, and he knew it was coming from Finn. His family was safe, and so was his friend. Brann took a moment to send back his thanks through the sliver of their bond before swimming deeper.

The land of Farriage Beach was only a half mile or so away, but the land dropped off next to the tall, flat side of the rocky mountain. The mouth of their cave was nearly fifty feet down, unreachable to anyone who couldn't swim as fast as the Daoine people, or hold their breath as long.

When Brann swam through the entrance, he was met with darkness. His eyes quickly adjusted as he made his way through the wide tunnel that had been carved out by the first of the Daoine settlers over forty years before.

He followed the sharp upturn that brought him to the large, calm pool inside. It spanned more than an acre, and there were many nooks carved into the rocks along the edges where people could climb up to sleep.

Along the higher parts of the walls were air vents, hidden in such a way that allowed for light and air to flow, but kept their secret from outsiders. In all their time there, no one had ever found them—human or remnant.

They had less fear of the sharks that occasionally found their way in than the possibility of man finding them. Especially the people on that storm ship.

"Is everyone inside?" Brann asked as he stepped out of the water.

A friend of his from when he was even younger than his little sister stepped forward. Her name was Caylee, and she was a few years older than him. "Everyone's inside. Finn helped to round everyone up. He's pretty incredible."

Brann smiled and nodded. "He sure is. I'm not sure his mom was too happy about it, though."

Caylee smiled. "Well, she helped, too. She probably knew Finn wouldn't leave until you were safe, and that she was going to have to help, if she wanted to get him out of here."

Brann laughed. "Probably."

There was a pause as she studied him. "How do you do it?"

"You're the second person to ask me that today," he said. With a shrug, he said, "I honestly don't know."

"Ever heard of the druids?" Lorelei said as she wandered over.

Brann shook his head, his face crinkling in confusion. "What's a durid?"

Lorelei laughed. "A *druid*. Grandfather told us about them after Ezekiel told *him*. I don't remember much. They are kind of like us, but totally different."

Brann's confusion only deepened. "Yeah. I get it. The same but totally different. That explains everything."

Putting her weight on one leg, and her hands on her hips, Lorelei said, "You know, for one so young, you're quite the smartass."

He shrugged. "We lived out in the open. We met a lot of people traveling to the beach, and they were *usually* pretty nice."

Her expression changed from stern to regretful as she realized what he meant by that. "Right. Well, anyway... Druids. Same but different. Instead of living in the water like we do, they live in trees, or something like that."

His eyes widened. "In trees? Why? They could fall out!"

Caylee laughed. "And I'm sure they'd look at us the same and ask how we don't drown."

"Excellent point," Lorelei said. "Like I said, I don't remember much. All I know is they are forest dwellers. But like you, they can talk to animals. Grandfather said that when a druid speaks, the animals listen, and when the animal speaks, the druid can somehow translate what those sounds mean."

His eyes widened. "Am I a durid?"

Lorelei shook her head as her eyes closed. "*Druid*. And I don't know. Maybe? I've never met one. And from what Grandfather said, we don't want to, either."

Brann's brows furrowed. "Why not? It sounds like they'd have answers for me. There are only a couple of other people in our tribes who can do what I do, and they understand it even less than I do."

"Druids are scary. Once, when your family was visiting, they mentioned meeting people from the Valley. Like you said, there aren't many of you. So when someone came, they couldn't wait to ask about the druids they had once heard about. Only the valley people told them how terrifying they are."

His mixed surprise and confusion only grew. "We are peaceful. How can forest people be so scary? Why?"

She shrugged. "I don't know. All I know is that the valley people said the druids were ruthless monsters. They killed any who ventured onto their land. They were fearless warriors and could kill a man with the flick of a wrist. They are proficient in weapons, and they could turn the forest animals on people. Hell, they could even turn a loyal dog to tear the throat from its master. I wouldn't be too excited to go looking for them, if I were you."

Brann sighed as he looked down, nodding. "I see. I thought… Well, I thought they might be able to teach me something. Tell me why I am the way I am. I want to know why my magic is different than most everyone else's. Maybe…"

"Maybe you could have saved your family if you'd been stronger?" Caylee asked.

He looked over, tears brimming in his eyes. It hadn't quite hit him until that moment just how scared he'd been after seeing that ship.

Brann nodded. "Yes."

"You saved *us*," Lorelei reminded him. "You saved *all* of us. Just now. You knew what that thunder was before any of us did. You knew what those clouds meant. If you hadn't been here, or if you would have hesitated, they might have seen us and killed all of us, too. You don't need some bastard druid to tell you how to use your gifts."

"But what if they aren't bastards?" he asked, and the Elder's eyes widened briefly at hearing him repeat her curse word. "What if that was just the word of one man? I'm sure to the people who live around the Farriage Coast, all of *us* are scary. But you can't tell me you wouldn't like to know how to actually defend yourself—to defend your family, if a fight came to you."

Lorelei stepped forward, wrapping the young boy in her arms. "You've been through far too much. You should sleep. Perhaps you'll feel better when you wake. The way you're talking… You worry me, Brann. We aren't fighters. We just aren't built for it. We are peaceful people, and we need to stick together."

Brann knew her words came from a place of fear, of worry. They came from a place of love and a desire to keep him safe. As an Elder, it was her job.

But that didn't change the way he felt.

His mind raced with the what ifs. *What if I hadn't acted so fast? What if I hadn't recognized the feel in the air? Would they have died, too? Not one of them can fight.*

Oh, they would try—just as his tribe had tried.

And they would fail.

The idea that there was another type of people out there with similar magic intrigued him. Knowing they were warriors intrigued him even more. It would take time… a *long* time… but one day, he would travel to the Valley and risk venturing into druid territory. Even if he ended up failing, Brann needed to take the chance.

He *never* wanted to feel so helpless again.

CHAPTER FOURTEEN

Arryn, Bast, and Cleo followed Zoe down the hall. Samuel and Cathillian had been left behind to sit with Corrine; they had protested, but Arryn argued it was part of their punishment for being late to the fight that morning.

Margit had arranged to have the captive taken to a cell for holding until everyone had been fed and well rested. Bast and Cleo had used far more magic than Arryn had, as they were still learning their limits in battle, and they needed time to recover.

Mostly, the Kemetian women used their power for building, not fighting as the men did. But when the monsters came, the women had taken up fighting as well. Bast and Cleo were already masters of their magic, but learning how to hold back in a fight to preserve energy was something new to them.

Still, though they were exhausted, they wanted to interrogate the woman. Like Arryn, they wanted to find out right away why she and the others had attacked Samuel's cabin. Waiting around and taking naps wasn't going to save lives if another attack was on its way.

"How have you been doing with your mental magic?" Zoe asked.

Arryn was glad Zoe's back was turned to her, because her expression betrayed her guilt. "Uh… great?"

Zoe laughed. "Nice try. I didn't need to be a mystic to hear the insecurity in that statement. You haven't been practicing, have you?"

Arryn sighed, feeling like a child being scolded. "No. Too many things have happened, and I had bigger things to focus on."

"Don't you think Hannah felt the same way?" Zoe asked. "She was overwhelmed with everything Ezekiel had to teach her, but she knew mental magic was the only way she would ever get things done. She knew it was a necessity. More than that, she was excited to learn."

"You know, I'm aware she's some big hero and all that, and I feel a debt of gratitude toward her for doing the job I should have been there to do, but at the same time, I'm getting real tired of people comparing me to her. I'm not Hannah. I don't know if I'll ever be Hannah."

Zoe stopped and turned, a smile on her face as a sense of compassion and warmth flooded through Arryn. The mystic was using her abilities to soothe the magician. "No. You're not Hannah. But the two of you have a lot in common, like your drive. I feel like we've had this conversation before. You worry too much. I'm not saying that you need to *be* Hannah; I'm not even saying that you need to be *like* her. I'm just saying that I know a little bit about where you're going, and if you're smart, you'll focus on mental magic."

Cleo all but pushed Arryn out of the way. "What does that mean? Do you mean south to the bandits? Or are you talking about Kemet?"

Zoe was quiet for a moment, obviously choosing her next words wisely. "Master Julianne returned from her journey, but left soon after. She has been sending mental messages back here, updating us on the situation. From what you, Cleo, and Bast have told me about where you're from and what's happening, I would have to say you're going up against the portal. Creatures from another world. Not monsters."

Arryn's eyes were wide, her jaw slack. She looked to her right to see that Cleo's face matched her own. There were so many questions swirling in Arryn's head at that moment, she scarcely knew where to begin.

"Another world?" Arryn asked. "You're serious? The monsters they've been talking about this whole time, the demons we are going to fight… This whole time, I thought they were mutated remnant or some shit like that. You're saying…"

Zoe nodded. "Margit has shown me images of what Julianne has seen, and they aren't remnant. They're nowhere near it. They come from the portals."

"You mean those long, tall cracks? The ones that look like they go nowhere?" Cleo asked.

"You've seen them?" Zoe asked.

"Yes," Bast said. "There is one several miles outside of Kemet. There aren't very many villages around us, so it seems they are drawn to our city. When we were last there, no one had seen anything directly inside our walls, but those who wandered outside were at great risk. We found pieces of some we'd lost, strewn across the desert as we rode our horses toward the sea. Then we crossed over to the land just south of here called the Farried Coast, or something like that."

"I believe it's 'Farriage'," Zoe said.

"Wait a minute," Arryn said. "The last time we spoke, you said Julianne was in the Madlands. Is that where she's gone now?"

Zoe nodded. "Yes. That's where the rift is, the portal like the one in Kemet."

Arryn shook her head, confusion all over her face. "Julianne sends mental messages all the way from the Madlands?" She had heard the words earlier, but had only just processed them.

Zoe smiled. "Like I said. You're gonna want to brush up on the mystical arts. Especially after you talk to Margit." She turned and resumed her walk down the hall.

Arryn turned first to Cleo with shock on her face. Then she turned to Bast with the same confusion. "Is she serious right now? She's just gonna say something like that and then turn around and walk away?"

"Sure am!" Zoe said in a singsong voice without missing a step.

Damn mystics, Arryn thought.

"I heard that," Zoe said. "And don't act like you're mad. You know you love me."

Arryn smiled. "You're lucky for that. Of course, I suppose I'm lucky you don't screw with my head. Wait… How did you get in my head without me knowing?"

Zoe sighed as she stopped and reached for the door handle on her right. "You were far too frazzled to notice. Again, you need a refresher course. You're letting your emotions control you, and your mind is wide open to anyone who wants to take a look inside—or do worse."

"Good to know," Arryn said. "Is our guest of honor behind that door?"

Zoe nodded. "In you go. I'll wait here; Margit is going to assist you. The woman has a surprisingly strong mental block, so it will take a bit more strength. I can do it, no problem, but Margit wanted the first crack."

A snarky smile pulled at the corner of Arryn's mouth. "I have a feeling *some*thing's going to be cracked by the time we get through with her."

Zoe smiled and rolled her eyes as she pushed the door open, gesturing for them to go inside.

"Welcome, ladies," Margit greeted. She stood with a certain level of power and respect in her old shoulders. "Given some of her colorful comments, I'm sure this will be a good time."

"Thank you for helping us with this," Arryn said. "There's no way we could have done this alone."

Margit quirked an eyebrow, giving the magician a knowing expression. "And whose fault would that be?"

Arryn looked at her incredulously. "Hey, I've already been raked over the coals. I've learned my lesson." She threw her hands into the air. "I relent. I'll focus more on mental magic. I didn't realize how important it was until today."

Margit gave her a curt, stern nod. "Good. Then we should begin. Just so you know, we do not make a habit of taking prisoners and barging into their minds. But there are exceptions. Like now, when innocent rearick lives are at stake, and the Temple is under attack."

Arryn nodded. "We know. We've spent enough time with Zoe to know what the mystics stand for."

Margit turned and stood behind the captive. The woman was tied to a chair, and Arryn couldn't help but notice she was in a far better condition than she herself would have left her in. But as the mystic said, they weren't in the business of torturing people.

"I'm going to ask you questions, and you're going to answer," Arryn began. "If you do not, Margit here will dive into your brain."

Get her talking. Once you ask a question, she won't be able to help the images that come to the front of her mind—even if she doesn't speak. She has a wall, but I should be able to break through if she focuses too much on you, Margit sent telepathically.

Arryn nodded. "You said a name earlier. Esmerelda. Is that the wife of the dead leader of the ex-Arcadian guards?"

The woman only smiled. "Esmerelda. I said a name, but that's all you're getting. And the old bat can try, but she'll never get through."

Arryn's expression became amused. "That 'old bat' could kick my ass, your ass, and the asses of the two beautiful but deadly women behind me. They are solid muscle, in case you hadn't noticed. So I'd be nice to the old bat."

"The next person that says 'old bat' is getting their entire identity erased," Margit warned.

Arryn cleared her throat and nodded. "Right. Anyway. Esmerelda. What does she look like? Oh, wait. I know. Short black hair. Super pale skin. Freckles across her face. Right?"

Medium height; long, curly, black hair; physically fit, Margit relayed. *Nice work giving a fake description. She mentally corrected you every time you said something wrong.*

The woman laughed. "You'll never get anything out of me. You can ask all you want."

Arryn smiled. "I think you're right. But I'm gonna ask questions anyway." She crossed her arms in front of her chest and sat on a chair across from the hostage. "I'm going to guess she is just like her husband—raging psycho, uses everyone around her to get what she wants, thinks she's better than all of you."

"You think you know her? You don't know shit. That *loving, doting* husband you keep talking about allowed his men to brutalize us. They beat us. Assaulted us in every way you could possibly imagine. We weren't the only ones; they did the same to her. When she found out he died?" The woman laughed. "Esmerelda saved us all."

That answer certainly caught Arryn off guard. She looked up to Margit, and the old woman's brows furrowed as she nodded.

Arryn focused back on the woman in front of her. "If you're victims, why spread that hate to other people? Why would you do to someone else what was done to you? You had the opportunity to take your terrible past and fight for those weaker than yourself. You may not be classically trained, but all of you know how to fight. You could use that to help instead of harm."

"Are you looking for something redeemable in me?" the woman asked.

Arryn wasn't exactly sure how to answer the question. After hearing what she had to say, and getting confirmation that she was telling the truth, the idea of killing the woman didn't exactly sit well with her.

Then again, neither did the woman's attempt to kill children.

"Part of me wants to make you realize the error of your ways. I want you to see what the world has to offer. Show you that you can suffer, can be in the deepest part of whatever hell you've been in, but still come out on top."

The woman smiled. "I'm sensing a 'but' there."

Arryn nodded. "That part of me is naïve. That part of me is the innocent child that will *always* be there. My *humanity*. Something the adult part of me knows you do not possess. If you had even an ounce, you never would've attacked children. I forgave the man who ruined my entire life and got my family killed because he had humanity left. But you? I've learned to listen to my gut, and my gut tells me there is no hope for you. Am I wrong?"

The woman shook her head. "No. You're not."

"I think we have everything we need here," Margit concluded.

The captive woman's brows furrowed as she struggled to turn and look at the older woman. "What do you mean? I didn't give you shit."

"On the contrary, you are quite an emotional one. You allowed your emotions to overpower reason. You became angry when thinking about your past, and it made you weak. Your barrier became thinner, and I was able to dive right in."

"Bullshit. You did no such thing. You're only saying that. It's all talk, but it's not going to work; I'm smarter than that, you old bitch," she said.

The captive woman cried out as tears almost immediately formed in her eyes, and her cries soon turned into screams.

Arryn's eyes widened as she watched Margit's white eyes

focus hard on her target. Then the captive fell unconscious, her head slumping to her chest.

"What the hell did you just do to her?" Arryn asked.

"I said the next person to call me an old bat was going to get it." Margit's expression was stern and unwavering, like that of a grandmother who had just caught a child red-handed.

"But she called you an old bitch, not an old bat. Not that I'm complaining. She deserved it," Arryn reasoned.

Margit nodded, looking over at the subdued young woman. "She called me an old something, and I warned her. I took her innermost desires, her terrible thoughts of what she wanted to do to you and to me, and I played them out in her mind."

Arryn smiled. "But I'm guessing she had the best role. The victim."

Margit shrugged. "It wasn't just us, Arryn. Their plans are dark. Esmerelda is far crazier than her husband. From what I've seen, she has enslaved the men and forces them to do her bidding. Not exactly saying I disagree; they deserve it, too. They deserve worse. But she's letting them live, and is using them to come for the Temple."

"What could they possibly want with the Temple?" Cleo wanted to know. "No offense, it's just… this is an old temple. It's beautiful, and there are many things to learn here, but I don't understand why bandits would want to take it."

"They want to take the mines," Margit said.

Arryn's eyes lit up. Everything was starting to make sense. "They wanted to take Craigston, but knew if they tried that the mystics would come down on them. Even if they managed to make it through the rearick—which was unlikely—they knew they'd have you guys to deal with."

Margit nodded. "They considered us the bigger threat and wanted to deal with us first. That's why your friend's house was attacked; it was close by. They came up that side of the mountain hoping to find a straight shot directly to us, but ran into you instead. I'm assuming the small group who went to Craigston were those who had gotten lost along the way."

"Do you think there will be another attack?" Bast asked.

Arryn nodded. "People like Esmerelda don't just go away. She will take that loss hard. If I know shitheads—and at this point, I feel like I really do—she is going to lose her mind over this. There *will* be another attack. We need to move south, quickly."

"Not without rest, you don't," Margit said. "And Arryn, you and I have a lot to discuss. You will want to stick around and hear what I have to say."

"So I've inferred," Arryn said.

"There won't be another attack tonight," Margit assured her. "You and I will speak, then you may all retreat for meditation. You'll have dinner tonight, and a full night's rest. After breakfast, you can leave."

"I didn't hear any option for a 'no' in there," Arryn said.

"Yeah, I don't think she gave one," Cleo said. "That's okay, though. I definitely need some sleep. Especially now that we have this out of the way. If you're confident the Temple is safe, we will take your recommendations."

Margit nodded. "Esmerelda will need time to form a new plan. It's hard to say if the injured have even returned to her yet to update her on the mission's failure."

"In that case," Cleo said with a hard pat to Arryn's back, "have fun. I get the impression she wants to speak to you alone, but don't think that lets you off the hook from telling us about whatever might affect our trip home."

Arryn smiled. "I'll update you as soon as I'm done here."

The girls smiled and made their way out of the room, shutting the door behind them.

Silent words were passed between Margit and the guards in the room, as they suddenly went to work removing their hostage.

Once they were gone, Margit turned to Arryn and smiled, lifting her wrist. On her wrist was a thin, silver bracelet. Though her arm moved, the piece of metal did not. It seemed to stay in place, as if attached to her.

"What's that?" Arryn asked.

"*This* is what you and I are going to be working on this afternoon. And prepare yourself; it isn't pleasant."

CHAPTER FIFTEEN

Arryn's eyes were wide as she stared at Margit. After sitting in total silence, listening to the old woman's every word, she felt like her mind might actually melt.

"Okay. Let me get this straight," she began. "That little bracelet right there somehow works with the nanocytes in our blood. The nanocytes are what give us our magic, and through that bracelet, my magic would be able to connect to anyone else who's wearing one. Is that right?"

Margit nodded. "But not just any magic—mystical magic. That means you actually have to get off your ass and practice."

Arryn looked at her with a disgusted expression. "Get off my ass? Lady, don't you realize I spend *most* of my time off my ass? All I ever do is train."

The mystic shook her head. "Child, please. Try to focus; do not use excuses with me. Let's not forget how you spent last night. All the drinking, and then the activities with—"

Arryn's eyes widened as she lifted her hands in the air. "I get it. I get it. *Dammit.* That's the last time I'm giving one of you full access."

"If you have time for all that, you have time for a little mental magic training. I didn't choose your path. You chose to be a warrior for the innocent. If you want to do that, and if you want to stop what's happening in Kemet, you will need every tool possible."

Arryn pointed to Margit's wrist again. "And that thing right there is going to help me?"

Margit nodded. "You will have a direct connection to Amelia, as well as to Julianne. The master mystic has been working to close the rift in Tahn. She will be able to guide you and help you with the creatures you will be dealing with. Otherwise, you will be going in blind."

Arryn let loose a heavy sigh. "This is unbelievable. *Another world.* What about the Queen Bitch? Does this mean…? Surely not, right? I mean, she couldn't possibly still be alive, right?"

"From what we know about Bethany Anne, she is still alive, and will one day return. It's impossible for me to know if she is even aware of the things that are happening here. Some pray to the Queen, others simply trust in her and believe she will return; many don't believe she exists at all. I personally believe she will be back one day.

"Right now, all we have are the Hannahs in the world. The Juliannes. The Arryns. She has blessed all of you, and because of that, you have the goddess-given duty of standing in her place until she returns. You must do the best you can and use all the tools you have been given to fight her fight, until the day she comes back to finish it."

Arryn's eyes widened, the weight of the mystic's words pressing down on her shoulders. She had never really thought of it in such a way before, but the old woman was right. Whether it was by Bethany Anne or by something else, she had not only been given power, she had been given an intense drive to use it to protect.

Her eyes lingered on the bracelet, then wandered up to meet Margit's. "I want it. Teach me how to use it."

Margit nodded. "This *will* require you to not be... *inactive*... with your training."

Arryn smiled, picking up on her word choice. She was a feisty, sarcastic, old woman, and Arryn enjoyed her immensely.

"No more *inactivity*. Promise."

With a sigh, Margit said, "Good. Now prepare yourself; like I said before, this hurts like hell."

Arryn's eyes widened. "No, you said it wasn't *pleasant*, not that it hurt like hell."

Margit shrugged. "I also chose to be nice and call you 'inactive' instead of 'a lazy brat'. I was trying to keep you at ease."

With a roll of her eyes, Arryn shook her head and extended her hand. "You really are a piece of work. But I adore you. You're still my favorite mystic."

Margit smiled. "We'll see how you feel after receiving the bracelet and going through my training."

***

Selena walked alongside Captain Seth as they made their way across the beach. It had taken quite a while, but she believed they had finally found the settlement they'd been looking for.

The lookout they'd sent ahead after landing reported seeing solid, semi-permanent tents set up all over. They grew larger the farther into camp they went. Toward the back, in the center, was the largest tent of all: from the looks of it, it would be able to hold two hundred or so people.

"Do you see that?" Captain Seth asked.

Selena nodded. "They have guards on the wall, but Tim didn't seem to think many more were inside. Judging by the number of people on the rampart, and the uncomfortable way they are shifting around, I would have to say he's right."

The captain nodded before motioning for everyone behind them to stop. "We'll try this the easy way."

With a dark smile, Selena said, "Yet I'm hoping for the hard way."

Selena and the captain made their way forward, stopping several yards away from gate. They both looked up to the guards manning the wall and gave a polite nod.

"I'm Captain Seth, and we want to see whoever's in charge here."

The guards looked at one another for a moment before looking back down at Selena and the captain. "What is your business here?" one of them asked.

Selena smiled. "We come from Holdgate. Well... At one time, we did. Have you ever heard of Storm Raiders?"

The guard's eyes widened as he nodded. "Not many people around here have heard of you, but we sure as hell have."

Captain Seth laughed. "I'll take that as a compliment. Now, we hear you have weapons; we'd like to take a look at those. If everything goes well, we have quite a lot of coin to offer in exchange for your best."

The guard they had been speaking to quickly nodded to one of the men on the edge of the wall. He quickly scurried away, no doubt going to speak to whoever was in charge.

"We are sending for Esmerelda. This shouldn't take long," the guard said.

Selena bit her lip, annoyed at having to wait. The captain brushed his hand against hers, signaling for her to keep calm. She took a deep breath and exhaled, forcing patience to return.

"Do you think they're going to let us in?" she asked.

Seth nodded. "I do. I don't hear a lot of clatter going on past the gate, and it's late evening. At this time of night, men would still be training, or at the very least, putting weapons away—we would be able to hear the sound of clanging metal. Also, I can smell meat cooking, but the scent is not overwhelming. That means there aren't many people to cook for. Something tells me they are down on warriors. If that's so, they'll take whatever we offer them; they will be desperate. So yes. I think they'll let us in."

Selena didn't reply. Instead, she alternated between nervously checking over her shoulder and keeping her eyes on the wall. Though her magic didn't work on land, she could still kick ass and beat the shit out of people with her staff, if the occasion called for it. She wasn't entirely convinced this wasn't a trap.

Nearly fifteen minutes had passed before the gate finally opened. When it did, a beautiful woman stood directly in the center, with four female guards standing on either side.

"Welcome, friends," she said. "My name is Esmerelda. Please, come inside. You must be hungry."

Selena and Captain Seth exchanged a look before turning back to Esmerelda.

"You may bring ten of your best men, but the rest stay outside." Esmerelda did not wait for a response. She simply turned and began to walk back inside.

Selena kept her eyes on the guards, her hand clenched tightly around her staff as the captain quickly chose ten of their best to accompany them. Once he returned, they followed Esmerelda through the encampment toward the large tent in the middle.

Looking around, Selena noted the report from their scout had been accurate. The captain had been right, as well. There weren't many people around. Some of the women were putting up weapons alongside the men, while others turned meat over a fire.

"This isn't quite the army I was expecting," Selena quietly admitted to Captain Seth.

He shook his head. "Me neither. I wonder what happened."

"Not to be rude," Selena said loudly enough for Esmerelda to hear. "But we came here to meet with a ruthless army. We were told the engineers were the best of the best from Arcadia. That the warriors were strong and there were many. What has happened?"

There was a long pause as Esmerelda continued to walk in

silence. Only a couple of her guards turned to look over their shoulders at Selena as she spoke.

It wasn't until they'd reached the tent and closed the flaps over the entrance that the bandit leader finally spoke. "It seems that I have an enemy. One that is quite determined to destroy what we have here."

Selena scoffed. "We know exactly what that's like. What happened?"

Esmerelda sat in a very large chair at the head of the room that resembled a throne. The only people in attendance were the three leaders, her guards, and the Raiders.

"Not long ago, a tribe of dark druids paid us a visit," she began. "They wanted to take the Dark Forest, but there was one young woman in particular they wanted to be rid of. Her name was Arryn. Now, for some time, we had been getting reports of our men being found dead. Some had even returned who had seen the murderer for themselves. What my husband was too stupid to realize was the descriptions were one and the same.

"The same young woman who was picking our men off was also the enemy of the dark druids. My husband partnered with them, went to war with them, and that same bitch killed him and the majority of our warriors. I just sent a large group north—into the mountains—to seize the Mystic Temple. What I didn't know was that Arryn would be there."

Selena shook her head. "And you lost all of your men."

Esmerelda laughed, but wasn't amused. "Not all of them, but certainly too many. I suspect she is on her way here now. This is not something we are prepared for, but we need to be. Therefore, I have a proposition for you."

Selena and Seth looked to one another. The captain turned his attention back to the woman, his brows furrowing. "I'm assuming you're about to ask us for help. And if that's so, tell me this... The dark druids could not defeat that girl. Your husband

and his men could not. You and your men could not. What could you possibly offer me to make me want to take her on?"

There was a pause as Esmerelda smiled, stood, and made her way down the steps to stand in front of the captain and his Storm Caller. "That mountain? It's full of amphoralds. The engineers use them to create magitech weapons. If we manage to kill that little bitch and take out the rearick and the mystics, we will have that mountain all to ourselves. That means an endless supply of amphoralds.

"We have a stockpile ready for sale. You can have all the weapons you can carry back to your ship, and you won't have to pay a single coin. More than that, you'll have access to our engineers to recharge the weapons when the crystals go bad. Not to mention, word spread fast about your little party up the coast. If you think for an instant that girl didn't hear about it, you're very wrong. She will soon be coming for you, too."

That certainly got Selena's attention. While she didn't like the idea of going to war with someone she had only just met, she couldn't deny it put them in a good position to come out ahead, if the girl truly had heard of their raid on the Farriage Coast.

"If she's right, we might need her help anyway," Selena said quietly to the captain. "She knows what we're going up against, but we don't. Getting a ship full of free weapons is just a bonus."

Captain Seth nodded. "Let us see the weapons first," he told Esmerelda decidedly. "I would like to see them before making my final decision."

She nodded. "As you wish. Follow me."

Selena narrowed her eyes as Esmerelda turned and began to walk away. She wasn't sure they could trust her, but something in her gut told her they wouldn't have much of a choice.

CHAPTER SIXTEEN

Arryn grimaced as she looked down at her wrist, fighting the intense urge to scratch. The last thing she wanted to do was remove the bracelet accidentally. In the words of Margit, it certainly hadn't been *pleasant* to get it. In fact, it hurt like hell.

The thin band of silver wrapped around her wrist, and the two sharp ends inserted into her skin and clipped together internally, where the pieces would have access to her blood and the nanocytes within.

Before the night had ended, Margit put her through a rigorous crash course in mental magic. Meditation was the only thing Arryn had kept up on—it was the only thing she had really found useful. While she had dabbled in the other stuff a bit, it certainly couldn't be considered practice.

And she had paid for it.

Dearly.

Arryn's head still hurt just thinking about everything Margit made her do. She had to force her way into Cathillian's mind, which had admittedly been much easier than when she'd had to do the same to Cleo. Samuel was right there to crack jokes about

Cathillian being an airhead. And of course, Arryn was there to join in on the fun.

Margit made Arryn practice for hours, and forbade her from using verbal communication until she departed from the temple. Margit had even gone so far as to go into Arryn's mind, compelling her to silence.

While Arryn knew she could speak, there was still no way for her to convince her brain to force her vocal chords to work. So, she was forced to spend the entire evening speaking telepathically.

But she hadn't been the only one to get in trouble.

Everyone else was able to talk with no consequence; however, anyone caught speaking to Arryn would have their ability revoked as well. They were allowed to speak her name to get her attention, but after that, the conversation was expected to be silent.

"You won't be here long, so I expect all of you to respect the need for Arryn to learn as much as possible in the short time you're with us. Any who do not will be forced to," Margit had told them.

Zoe had been in charge of keeping the rest of the group honest because Margit was completely focused on Arryn. If the Arcadian druid wanted to speak to anyone directly, she was expected to call them out telepathically. Only then were her friends allowed to respond, also telepathically.

As the night droned on, the challenge became harder. Arryn was expected to keep constant telepathic connection to all of her friends. Their ability to verbally get her attention was taken away, and she had to listen for them to speak to her directly through the link.

By the end of the night, Samuel was the only one left with the ability to speak. "Sorry, lads and lasses. I ain't about ta lose this one. It's bad enough I got several people magickin' in me head. I don't need one going in an' messin' shit up."

The entire night had been hell for Arryn—and for everyone else in her group, if she were honest with herself. But it had worked. As much as she hated to say it, the plan had worked.

She sure as hell wasn't a master like Zoe or the famous Julianne, but she walked out of that temple the next morning knowing how to use telepathy, the bracelet, and how to strengthen her mental barrier to keep even a mystic out.

Well, until they really started trying.

Arryn knew she had a long way to go, and that it would be a while before she could do many of the things she had seen Zoe do, but the thought of learning how to do all three forms of magic excited her.

"That *really* looks uncomfortable," Cathillian said as he rode up next to her, Echo soaring close by—a little *too* close for Arryn's comfort.

Arryn shook her head at the playful raptor before going back to staring at the piece of metal clipped into her skin, trying not to scratch at it. The surrounding area was tender and red, with a dried drop of blood on each side. "Yeah, it isn't exactly a good feeling. It would be fine, if it didn't itch so badly."

He nodded. "Yeah, it's not like we can heal it or anything. Your body is just going to have to adjust."

"Are we allowed ta be talking to her righ' now?" Samuel asked. "I don't know how far those mystics can reach, but I don't feel like challengin' 'em."

Arryn smiled. "Relax, ya big chicken. We're away from the temple; you can talk to me. Just like I can tell you out loud that Margit gave me a detailed schedule of things I need to do every day."

"Sounds like something you would do for a child," Cleo said.

Arryn turned her head to see the woman smiling at her while riding on her horse. "Do you want to get pushed off the mountain? Because that's how you get pushed off the mountain."

Cleo laughed. "You valley folk are a sensitive bunch, aren't ya?"

Arryn laughed. "Cathillian maybe. I'm never sensitive about anything." There was a brief pause, and Arryn could feel all eyes on her just before she burst with laughter again. "I couldn't hold that in for very long."

"Uh, guys? I think we might've made a wrong turn," Samuel said.

"What do you mean *'a wrong turn'*? You're the native here." Arryn and Snow trotted faster to catch up to the rearick.

"I spent me days in the mine an' traveling back an' forth ta the city. I ain't been this side o' the mountain in a long time. Don't get mad at me, lass."

Snow bent down, and Arryn slid off the side. The trail had come to an abrupt end, and so had their ability to move safely down the mountain. Adding insult to injury, Echo flew past and landed on a large rock at the bottom of the mountain, looking up at Arryn.

Little shit, Arryn thought with amusement.

Only ten feet away from where the group stood was nearly a straight shot down. One hundred feet or so to the right, the plummet would land them directly in the water—from what she could see, it was relatively deep, too. Directly in front of her, however, would be a several-hundred-foot drop onto a beach.

"Bast, Cleo," Arryn said. She heard footsteps behind her as the twins approached, and she told them her idea. "I can teleport myself and probably two of the horses; Cathillian and Corrine can use vines to descend, and they can take Samuel along, as well. Snow and Dante might be able to find a way down on their own. Do you think you can get yourselves and the other two horses down?"

Cleo looked over the edge, a smile spreading across her face. Her brown eyes turned blue as she turned back to Arryn. "That's sand."

Arryn eyed her suspiciously. "Yes? And that means…"

A hand clapped down on Arryn's back, and she turned to see Bast smiling, her eyes also blue. "We have a better idea. Why don't you, Cathillian, and Corrine use vines to create a sling for the horses. You should be able to soothe them before lowering them, yes?"

Arryn thought for a moment. "I suppose we could. I was worried wrapping vines around them might make them skittish and uncomfortable, but working together, the three of us should be able to keep them calm."

"Good! Then we'll take care of the rest." Bast winked before placing her foot on the edge of the cliff and jumping hard.

Cleo was only a breath behind her. Each woman soared twenty feet out before plummeting toward the beach.

"What the hell are you doing?!" Arryn shouted after them.

"I knew they were crazy, but I didn't know they were suicidal," Cathillian said from beside her.

Sand began to whirl over the beach, then lifted into the air to catch them mid-fall. The twins landed safely on their feet, each of them looking up and giving a wave.

"They're from the desert," Corrine reminded the druids. "Sand is what they know best."

Arryn smiled. "I hadn't thought about that. Is anyone else intimidated by them, or is it just me? They are amazing."

The sand on the beach circled again as the twins began to move in tandem. They swirled their arms in the air, moving much like dancers would, and the sand lifted from the beach, twisting through the air until it rose to the very edge of the cliff.

Bast shouted something from below, but Arryn couldn't hear her. "What?" she shouted back.

Once again Bast shouted, but Arryn still couldn't make it out.

"Um…" Cathillian said, giving a gentle tap to her temple.

"Oh! Right." her eyes flashed, only a gentle cloudiness

appearing around the edges of her pupils as she looked over the edge of the mountain.

I can't hear you from up here, she told the twin.

Look at the shape. Set fire to it. We can heat the sand, but to do so while using as much magic as we are to control this, we would deplete ourselves, Bast responded.

Arryn studied the shape the sand had taken. It was a snaking half-circle, tall at the edges and slightly rounded at the bottom, that reached from the ground up to the top of the cliff where the rest of the party stood.

Her lips quirked as blackness began to spread from the cloudy parts of her eyes. She stepped in front of the sand. With a flick of her wrists, blue fire surrounded her hands, and she lowered them to the cliff's edge.

She thrust her hands forward then, sending the fireballs spreading out in a line over the sand and racing downward. The line spiraled all the way to the ground, creating a thick, solid glass slide.

You probably wanna cool that off before you send anyone down, came Bast's voice.

Arryn smiled, realizing she hadn't lost connection to Bast while casting other magic. *Will do.*

Standing, she turned toward the others with a smile. "Is anyone else as excited as I am to go down that thing?"

Corrine had a large smile as she stared at it. "Can I go first?"

"They're a couple of showoffs," Cathillian decided with a shake of his head and an amused smile. "Pretty damn impressive."

Arryn nodded. "I barely used any magic conjuring that fire. The amount of energy it would've taken to teleport myself and only two of those horses would have been incredible. And the twins didn't have to move heavy earth, either. All in all, this was a pretty good idea."

Cathillian turned, gesturing toward the horses. "Shall we?"

Arryn nodded before her eyes flashed green. She took a deep

breath as she and Cathillian walked a few feet over and urged the horses to come to them. Along with Corrine, they soothed each of the four large animals before wrapping their midsections in vines. Then they strapped leaves over their eyes, forcing them closed so the animals wouldn't be able to see just how high in the air they were.

Even though they had the ability to calm the horses, Arryn knew their primary focus would be on getting them safely to the ground.

As they lowered the horses, new vines burst from the face of the mountain, wrapping around the animals as they descended. Toward the end, the horses became restless, bucking a bit against their bonds. But soon, they were safely on the ground, and Bast and Cleo got to work freeing them.

On top of the mountain, Arryn walked over to the slide and knelt down. The glass was still a bit warm to the touch, but it had cooled very quickly during the time it had taken to lower the horses.

"What do you think?" Cathillian asked.

She thought for a moment. "It's not hot, but any part of our skin that touches it could be rubbed raw." She stood, placing her hands on her hips as a smile spread on her face.

"So… I'll ask again. What do you think?"

"Get your sleeping bags," she said. Cathillian opened his mouth to protest, but she shook her head and pointed off to the side. "I removed yours and Samuel's before we sent the horses down."

His eyes narrowed. "You already knew you were going to send us down like this, didn't you?"

She nodded excitedly. "Yep! But when you asked me what we were going to do, I was estimating just how killy and deathy it could be."

He smiled. "'Killy and deathy'?"

"I ain't likin' the sound of either of those, lass," Samuel said.

Corrine jumped up and down and clapped her hands, the white rabbit calmly hopping out of the way before he was trampled. "I do, I do! It'll be fun! If we fly out, we can just use vines to catch ourselves."

Cathillian laughed. "Except the vine would come out of the side of the mountain, wrap around you, and drop you in an arc before smashing you against the rocks."

Arryn shrugged. "Head trauma, max. We can heal that."

Cathillian looked at her incredulously. "The scary part is that I know you're serious."

"We have the best magic out of anyone. We can do crazy, killy, deathy things and heal ourselves when it goes bad," Arryn said nonchalantly.

Arryn heard shuffling and turned to see Corrine now holding the rabbit and pulling her sleeping bag from the pack on Dante's back.

"Look at her. She so excited!" Arryn pointed out to Cathillian. "Don't kill the little girl's dreams."

"Killing her dreams is the least of my worries," Cathillian said with amusement, though his arms were crossed in defiance. "I'm more concerned with killing *her*. You're supposed to be her role model and keep her safe. Remember?"

Arryn pointed to the slide. "Look. The twins already anticipated all of that. The edges are curved up and inward, so when we go around the turns, our bodies will probably move up the sides, but the top edges will keep us from flying out. Now, stop being a wuss. I'll go first to prove it's safe."

Cathillian's physical stance became even more stern, something that she wasn't used to seeing from him unless he was truly worried, but she stopped him with a gentle hand on his chest.

Relax. I'll be fine. And I would never put any of you in danger—you know that.

His eyes closed, and he let out a short sigh. Finally, he nodded. *Please be careful.*

Arryn quickly made her way over to Snow and retrieved her sleeping bag. Then she ran to the edge of the slide, unrolled the bag, slipped inside, pulled it up to her shoulders, and sat down. An excited Corrine stood waiting just behind her, sleeping bag in one hand and a seemingly nervous rabbit in another.

"Wait until I'm all the way down at the bottom," Arryn told her. "I want to make sure it's completely safe. Keep Fluffenstuffs in your lap."

Corrine nodded, the beaming smile never leaving her face. Arryn faced forward, squinting her eyes a bit as the sun glared through the glass. Placing her hands on the edges, she pushed off hard.

She squealed in excitement as she took off down the slide, rounding each turn faster than the last. She couldn't remember the last time she had ever had that much fun, and it made her want to climb right back to the top and do it again.

When she reached the bottom, she shot off the end like a rocket, skidding across the sand and rolling a bit as she came to a stop.

She laughed loudly as she untangled herself from the sleeping bag and climbed out. She began to knock all of the sand off of her, even trying to dust it out of her hair, but she knew it was pointless.

"Fun, yeah?" Bast asked.

"Bitch and Bastard! Your way was *so* much more fun! I want to do it again." Arryn laughed again as she picked up her sleeping bag and shook the sand out.

She walked over to the twins and placed a flat hand just above her eyes to shield them from the sun. She could see Cathillian looking over the edge.

That was the best fucking thing ever! You have to do it! Send Corrine down first.

She could almost feel his eyeroll from where she stood.

Sending her now. She's been waiting very impatiently ever since she heard your first scream, he sent back.

Arryn could feel the slight twinge of a headache forming, and she knew it was because she still wasn't used to the mental magic — especially across the current distance.

A loud scream—followed by an even louder *"YEAAAH!"*—echoed through the air. Arryn laughed as she listened to Corrine howl and giggle all the way to the bottom. Because she wasn't as heavy as Arryn, the little girl didn't have quite the rough landing the druid had, but it was still funny. The rabbit leapt out of her arms and stayed close as the little girl climbed to her feet.

"How did you like that?" Arryn asked her when she was upright.

"Can we please do that again?" Corrine asked.

"Don't worry, kid," Cleo said. "When we get to Kemet, you can slide all day long. We have hundreds of those all over. While we're building, that's how we get from high up on the pyramids back down to the ground. It's much easier than climbing or using ladders."

Corrine's eyes widened. "I can't wait!"

"Ah, *feck!*" Samuel screamed.

Arryn knew Cathillian must have sent him next, and she began laughing hysterically. The rearick cursed all the way to the bottom before getting dumped out onto the sand and rolling several times.

He launched into a tirade of curse words she had never heard while trying to stand and shake his sleeping bag free, and Arryn promptly went weak in the knees and fell scream-laughing to the ground.

"Ah, ye think this is funny, do ye?" he asked.

Arryn could hardly breathe, let alone answer his question. She only nodded as she rolled over to her hands and knees, slowly bringing herself once again to a standing position.

Suddenly Dante shot out the end of the slide, knocking

Samuel over again. He landed so hard in the sand, his head dipped down, and his feet went up in the air, earning howling laughter out of everyone.

Arryn heard screaming from on top of the cliff, and she looked up to see Cathillian pointing at Samuel and laughing.

Once again, Samuel struggled to his feet, cursing in what sounded like a different language. He turned to Dante—who seemed to have more decency than the humans—pointed, and grumbled something unintelligible before stomping off.

Dante's ears twitched, and he moved out of the way just before his mother appeared from the end of the slide. Unlike her cub, she had prepared for the landing. Like the graceful cat she was, she leapt to her feet at the last moment and ran as she hit the sand, gradually slowing to a stop.

Any day now, Arryn urged Cathillian.

She heard loud yelling, then screaming, and then he shot out the end, flipping his long hair back while wearing a broad smile. "Fuck! That was so fun!"

"See? I told you!" Arryn said.

"Uh, guys?" Samuel said.

Arryn sighed, her smile still on her face. "Sam, last time you said that, we ran out of path. What is it—"

She turned to see a large group of people standing on the beach, eyes glowing a beautiful aqua color as they focused their magic directly on the druid and her group.

CHAPTER SEVENTEEN

Brann watched from the edge of the water, curious about what might happen. His heart raced, and his mind wasn't far behind.

The Elders had heard loud shouting through the air vents and, to Brann's surprise, they rushed to investigate. At first, he had worried it was the people from the storm ship, but then he realized the sounds were coming from on top of the mountain.

He had snuck out after the Elders left and made his way to the edge of the beach, where the land dropped off and the water became very deep. The Elders had hidden themselves to watch, so Brann did the same.

He watched excitedly as two women jumped from the edge and called the sand for a soft landing. He watched them create a massive structure, and looked on as each newcomer slid down, one after the other.

But his real interest lay with the first girl who had come down.

Even from her place at the top of the mountain, he could sense her magic. He had watched her and her friends lower the horses to the ground with vines, and now he could see large cats, bigger than anything he had ever seen, snuggling up next to her.

They have to be druids, he thought to himself.

As he watched, he found himself wondering if they truly were monsters. From where he sat, he could see them laughing and playing, joking with one another. Deep down, he could feel no bad intentions coming from them.

Then again, he could also see swords, bows, battle axes, and knives. They were heavily armed, and each of them had the body of a warrior—even the girl who looked younger than him.

As his distant relatives approached, he could feel their magic beginning to flare up. He was a little more than shocked to see them actually moving forward, instead of fleeing. Perhaps Lorelei had taken his words to heart.

"Who are you, and what do you want?" Lorelei demanded as she stepped forward.

The young woman he had seen slide down first stepped forward, her hands out to her sides in a peaceful manner.

She must be the leader.

"My name is Arryn. I'm not sure who you are, but if you don't mean us any harm, I can assure you we don't mean you any."

"We don't see a lot of people this way, and there have been a lot of things going on lately. State your business with the Farriage Coast," Lorelei said sharply.

"We meant to descend the mountain, but not here. We made a wrong turn. We are hunting a group of bandits who have been terrorizing the Arcadian Valley. Yesterday, they attacked innocent children on the mountain. We need to stop them before they hurt anyone else," the woman said fearlessly.

What? They don't seem so bad... Brann's breath caught in his throat as her eyes turned directly on him. From where he sat, he could see the look of amusement on her face as she gave a wink. Somehow, Lorelei didn't seem to notice.

"Bandits? Are you talking about the storm ship?" Lorelei asked.

He watched the druid turn her attention back to Lorelei. "Storm ship? No. From what we've been told, there's an encampment further down the coast, with hundreds of warriors. They were Arcadian Guard, before the city fell and they were forced out. Now they craft weapons and sell them to the highest bidder."

Lorelei turned to her brother. "That must be where the storm ship was heading."

"What storm ship?" the druid woman asked. "Maybe we can help."

Brann jumped out of the water, rushing forward. Several arms reached out for him when he was noticed, but he managed to dart from every one of them and make his way to the front.

"I saw them. I saw them kill everyone," he blurted.

The young woman's eyes stared into his, her face scrunching in what looked like sympathy. "Tell me everything."

"I was swimming when the ship came, and they called storms to make the ship faster, and their thunder doesn't sound like normal thunder; it doesn't feel like a normal storm, and there was something cold and dark about it, and by the time I reached land, they had killed most of my village, including my parents, and I only managed to save my little sister." He inhaled deeply, having explained it all in a single breath.

"You were very brave to do what you did," the woman told him. "I guess we were meant to find you; you seem unused to outsiders, and we have never been this far south. If you can trust me, though, we can help you." The young woman smiled, and Brann found himself lost in her charm.

His heart began to race again as a question touched the tip of his tongue. All he had to do was force it out.

Taking another deep breath, he asked, "Are you druids?"

Arryn smiled and nodded. "I was born in Arcadia, but I was

raised in the Dark Forest. The tall, blonde guy behind me is definitely a druid, though."

"Brann, get back," Lorelei said, her voice low and full of warning.

Arryn's head was still tilted downward from talking to Brann. Only her eyes lifted as she studied Lorelei. "We do not mean you harm. I have offered you our assistance."

Lorelei's brother spoke, and Brann turned his head to see him step forward. "We've heard about your kind. We've heard what you people do when innocents cross over your borders. You're ruthless. Cruel." He looked down to Brann, his face stern. "Get. Back."

The boy shook his head. "If she wanted me dead, I already would be."

"She hasn't attacked you because she knows she's outnumbered. That's the only thing keeping you safe right now," Lorelei said.

"Not to stir the pot here," Arryn said. "But what's keeping him safe is my good heart. Not your numbers. My parents were murdered by a tyrant when I was around his age. I've dedicated my life to helping those who are too weak to help themselves. Believe me when I say that being outnumbered is not a threat."

"How the hell are we supposed to trust that? We've heard the stories. We know what you're capable of. If you were being honest, you wouldn't have need for all those weapons," Lorelei spat. Brann saw her eyes begin to glow, but he was too slow to stop her.

Her hands thrust forward, pulling water from the air and wrapping it around the druid's head.

Brann turned, eyes wide in fear. *I believe her. Why can't they?*

Arryn's eyes flashed black, and the water evaporated almost immediately. With a flick of her wrist, Brann was flung back against a large rock. While it hurt, he knew she had been gentle. His head had somehow been protected—the levitation completely controlled. He couldn't move; as he watched her entire body flex, creating a blast of wind to knock his entire family to the sand, he understood why.

She hadn't wanted to hurt him.

The speckling of clouds above them began to darken as the wind whipped around the druid. Her eyes turned green around the irises as she lifted her hands out to her sides. She pulled downward, teasing water from the air and turning it into shards of ice.

Brann's family gasped, clinging to one another as the druid swung her arms forward and clapped her hands together. The ice sailed through the air, but abruptly stopped before impact. The shards hung, motionless, as Lorelei slowly opened her eyes and risked a look.

"Like I said before. It is my good heart." The young woman dropped her hands, and the ice immediately melted into water and rained down on his family, as her eyes returned to normal. "You are afraid of us because of things you've only been told. Don't let prejudices and fear control you, or you will prove yourselves no better than those you fight against."

Brann was finally able to move, and relief flooded through him as he watched his family rise to their feet. He slid down the rock and ran over to Arryn.

"When you called your magic, the sky went dark," he said. "Can you use magic like they can?"

"Storm magic is very difficult. In the Dark Forest, only a very few can call it: the Chieftain, his daughter Elysia, his grandson Cathillian—that pretty boy right back there—and me. But way, *way* up north, there is a village of Storm Callers. I don't know much about them, but I heard once that they were having troubles of their own, with some of the people on the ships being bad," she answered.

"Sounds like we found one of the bad ships," Lorelei noted. "Look, I'm sorry. We're peaceful people; our tribe stays clear of outsiders, but Brann's wasn't so lucky, and their fate has put all of us on edge. We've realized the time has come to fight."

"Our tribe believed in being open and kind to everyone, so we built our homes on the beach… Not having a good place to hide was what got everyone killed," Brann said.

Arryn nodded. "Why don't we all sit down and talk? We can tell you about ourselves and where we're from, and you can all tell us more."

"It kind of sounds like they're water druids," Cleo interjected. "Is there any such thing?"

Cathillian shrugged. "I've never heard of anything like that, but then again, it wasn't until recently that I even left the Dark Forest."

Brann smiled. He had been wondering the same thing ever since he first heard about the druids of the Dark Forest. *Now I get to find out.*

CHAPTER EIGHTEEN

Arryn still felt a bit shaky from the initial meeting of the Daoine people. She knew they were innocent by the story the boy had told, but they weren't convinced of her innocence. Hurting them had certainly been the last thing she wanted to do, and scaring them had been just below that on the list.

Just before Lorelei had attacked her with water, no doubt hoping to incapacitate her and potentially drown her, Arryn could feel intense fear rolling off of her in waves. It wasn't anger or malice that had driven Lorelei to attack her. It had only been a knee-jerk reaction in an attempt to save her family.

When Arryn had realized things were about to get bad, she grew worried that the rest of her group would attack in her defense. If that happened, there would be no chance for peace. So she sent out an order.

Stay back.

It wasn't lost on her just how much using the mental magic had assisted her. Had she yelled that same order, Cathillian and the others might have assumed she was talking to the Daoine. But because she was able to project her thoughts directly, there was no misunderstanding.

She hated to admit it, but she would have to thank Margit for that later.

The little boy showed a deep curiosity in her. More than that, he trusted her. She could feel in her gut that there was something special about him, and it seemed to be what drew him to her.

"Why do you want to help us?" Lorelei asked.

They had spent the previous two hours sitting on the beach and talking. They first discussed what had happened in the Daoine village; Arryn then took the time to explain who they were, where they were from, and why those rumors about druids being dangerous had been spread. To further earn Lorelei's trust, Arryn explained how they had come to be in their current position.

"There is a very large part of me that can't just stand by while people suffer. Ever since I was ten, I had big dreams of going back to Arcadia and finding the man responsible for killing my parents and destroying so many other lives. When I finally got there, someone else had already done it. But the city was still far from safe.

"We freed the city from its lingering threats, and since then, it's been one journey after the next. We headed back to the Dark Forest to save our home, and by that time, Bast and Cleo showed up needing help in their own part of the world, and the bandits had proven themselves to be quite the problem, as well. So once we fought the battle in the Dark Forest, we came searching for the bandits and found you. Once this is all finished, we will go on to Kemet. From there, who knows?" Arryn replied.

"It really has been one shit-show after another, hasn't it?" Cathillian asked. "I hadn't thought about it much until you just laid it out like that."

Arryn laughed. "Yeah, it really has been. But it's been fun. And look at all the people we've helped along the way."

"I have a question," Brann ventured.

Arryn turned to face him, a smile on her face. "Ask away."

"Can you teach me to be like you? I want to be strong."

She could see the determination on his face as he spoke, and it warmed her. "You managed to save your little sister in the middle of something I can't even imagine. As bad as things were when I was a kid, I didn't see anything compared to what you have," Arryn replied.

"But I don't feel like I did much. I'm glad I saved her; I don't want anyone to think I'm not. But I could've done more. I *know* it," he said, looking down at the ground.

"Brann, you have to stop blaming yourself," Lorelei said. "You haven't stopped saving us since you got here."

"It's not enough," he said.

"It'll never be enough," Arryn said. "Trust me, I know. This is what drives me every day. I assume my friends feel the same way, otherwise, I doubt they would be able to stand being around me for very long."

"How do you handle it? It seems like you go out on adventures every day and make yourself useful," he observed.

She smiled again. "I just try to do what I can, all the time. My mom taught me magic. Physical magic." Arryn's eyes flashed black as she flicked her wrist, and a red and orange fireball formed in her hand. "She was one of the best magicians in Arcadia, and she taught me. I was ten when she died, and I still didn't know a whole lot."

Brann's eyes were bright with the glow of the fire and the excitement of what Arryn had to say. "So how did you become who you are now?"

Arryn closed her fist, and the fire disappeared, her eyes returning to their normal brown. "Practice. I practiced what my mother taught me every single day in the Dark Forest. I wasn't able to do a whole lot because I was surrounded by nature magic users, but I still perfected the things that she taught me."

"It wasn't until she met Samuel that she became serious about learning magic," Cathillian interjected.

Arryn laughed. "I would like to say he's wrong, but he's really not. It's not that I didn't *want* to learn—I was just a scatterbrain, as the Chieftain called me. I couldn't focus. I always had a million thoughts in my head at once, and it limited my ability to practice. But I still got up every day and trained in hand-to-hand combat with Cathillian, and in magic with the Chieftain and Elysia."

"What changed?" Lorelei asked.

"Samuel fought in the battle against Adrien to save Arcadia. He told us what happened, and it reminded me that I had purpose. It reminded me that I had made promises—not only to myself, but to my parents. I think I had just become afraid I would never be good enough, and I let it stunt my progress.

"After that, I trained my ass off, completed the trials that would allow me to leave the Dark Forest, and then I went back to Arcadia. Cathillian even took the trials with me so he could make sure nothing happened to me," she said with a smile.

"Well… you wouldn't have let me, if you'd had any say. But the Chieftain wouldn't allow you to go otherwise," Cathillian said.

Arryn laughed. "Yeah. He kind of forced you on me."

"What about her?" Lorelei asked, pointing at Corrine. "She seems very young to be traveling with a group such as yourselves."

There was a pause as Arryn looked over at Corrine snuggling Sir Fuzzypants and winked. "She's eight and she has a very long, troubled story. She wasn't always part of our tribe; we adopted her, and there isn't a day that goes by I'm not grateful for it. She might be young, but she has saved our lives many times. Mine especially."

Arryn looked to Brann. "You feel like there is something out there calling your name; I get that. Maybe you and Corrine should talk. She came from nothing: her parents wanted nothing to do with her, and she was forced to live high in the trees to avoid her own people, because they would hurt her whenever they saw her. Throw things. Kick her. Insult her."

"But then I met Arryn," Corrine chirped in a voice that warmed the druid's heart. It seemed her past no longer affected her as it once did; even the mention of it could not break her smile. "After getting to the Dark Forest, I learned how to grow things and even how to heal people."

Brann's eyes lit up as he sat up on his knees. "You can heal people?"

Corrine nodded. "We all can. It's nature magic."

Brann smiled. "I can heal, but it's not really on purpose. I don't understand how it works. I healed a newborn dolphin once after it was attacked by a shark, and we've been best friends ever since."

Arryn's eyes widened. "You're bonded to a dolphin?"

"Bonded?" he asked.

She laughed. "Yeah, we have a lot to talk about. Why don't you and Corrine go play? She's an excellent teacher—maybe she can teach you how to heal on command. You already know how to do it, so doing it on command won't be much of a stretch. She can also tell you all about bonds, physical training, and anything else you want to know."

Brann looked to the Elders. "Can I? Please?"

Lorelei hesitated, then smiled. "Maybe you can show her Finn. I'm sure she'd enjoy meeting him. But… I think you know where you're not allowed to go."

Arryn looked down at her hands and fidgeted with them to hide the cloudiness in her eyes. She had accidentally looked into the boy's brain earlier, just before the scuffle. He had a wide-open mind, and it almost screamed at her.

Risking a look again, she saw that he understood exactly what Lorelei meant: she didn't want him to talk to Corrine about where they hid, and they certainly weren't allowed to go there.

Thoughts of the cave were right on the surface of his mind, so she backed out before she saw something they didn't want her to see. She had only looked out of worry for Corrine; she didn't want to completely violate their privacy.

As she pulled back, her eyes returned to normal, but there was a dull headache pounding away in her forehead. She inhaled deeply and exhaled slowly as she focused it away.

The kids jumped up and ran toward the water, laughing and talking about the dolphin as they went.

"Now that they're gone," Lorelei began, "I think we should come up with a plan to deal with the bastards on the ship."

Arryn smiled. "I couldn't agree more."

CHAPTER NINETEEN

Mariana had just finished bringing the scout boat back to their ship, using only enough power to move it through the water. They had decided to sail wide, steering clear of the coast to avoid being seen by Selena and her crew. Any true storm magic would be sensed by the rival master Storm Caller, and Mariana would risk losing the Raider ship all over again.

She couldn't allow that to happen.

Instead of risking discovery, upon leaving the destroyed Daoine village on the Farriage Coast, they had sailed several miles out to sea using only gentle winds. It had taken much longer, but when they headed southwest, she could still sense Selena's magic, lingering in the air.

Every time, Mariana and Captain Veren had opted to rush in, and every time, the other ship fled before they could get too close. So far, subtlety wasn't working in their favor.

"We are about five miles west of them," Smiley reported. "There is a small cove just out of sight of our ship. I wanted to check it out, so I rowed the rest of the way there. It looked like it could be the one that old woman described to us. From where I landed, they were about three miles up the coast."

"What did you see?" Veren asked.

"There was a large encampment built against an easily scalable mountain, with a large barrier around everything else; there were over a hundred tents. I saw Selena walking with another woman. The captain was with his men and seemed to be training with others in the camp," Smiley said.

"Hmm... I wonder what they are training for?" Mariana mused. "Did it look like they had any magitech weapons?"

Smiley shook his head. "No. And I recognized all the faces of the crew; I think they were training the people in the camp. They seemed to be on the offensive."

Mariana looked at him. "That's even worse. Maybe they came to some kind of an arrangement—training in exchange for a better cost on weapons."

Captain Veren shook his head. "Think about that for a second. If the captain's crew could easily overtake the others, if the others were that weak, the crew would have no reason to pay for the weapons. They only pay for what they can't take. There's something more going on there, but I don't have a clue what it could be."

Mariana sighed. He was right. They were Raiders; if they were stronger than the men and women in that camp, they would simply take what they wanted. They sure as hell wouldn't be training them to make them stronger.

"I need to get on land and see this for myself," Mariana said.

"You think that's wise?" the captain asked.

"Selena might be able to sense you," Smiley warned her.

Mariana shook her head. "No, she won't. I'm not going to use any of my magic. We're going to row the whole way. Besides, we need to make sure that kid arrived safely. I gave that woman at the destroyed village my word."

ARRYN, Bast, and Cathillian moved quietly up the coast with Lorelei. Samuel and Cleo were left behind, just in case anything went wrong, and Corrine and Brann needed protection.

"We saw the ship coming down the coast. They would've reached us within an hour if they had continued in that direction; that makes me think they docked somewhere in between," Lorelei said.

"Well, I sense a nosy little rabbit trailing behind us, so we're going to put him to work," Arryn said as she turned her head.

Trailing close behind was Not-Rodney the bunny, his little brown feet slowly trudging through the sand. Echo was ordered to stay behind and guard the others. It would also have been very difficult for her to remain unseen high in the sky.

"Wait a second…" Arryn said, making her way back to the rabbit. She knelt down and lifted his front paw. "These were white on the mountain. Now they're brown. Cathillian, have you seen this?"

Cathillian knelt next to Arryn and picked up the rabbit. "I think Whiskers has gotten a little chunkier. And yeah, his feet are definitely a different color. There isn't even a hint of the green stain left." He paused. "You haven't bonded with a *third* animal, have you?"

Arryn shook her head. "No. Besides, he's always shoved up Corrine's ass. And did you call him *just* Whiskers? Nothing else with it? Is that really all you got? That's almost worse than 'Rodney'. *Almost*, but not quite. Still… That's just offensive."

Cathillian's eyes narrowed. "He's definitely bigger—not much, but enough. His fur is changing colors, and he's been attached to Corrine. What do you think that means?"

Shock registered on Arryn's face, and she shook her head. "But why would he come with me, if he's bonded to her? Do you really think it's true?"

Cathillian shrugged. "She probably has no idea and told him to go with you. I know she had hoped to make the wolf her familiar, but it seems Fluffy here beat that bond to the punch. I can't know for sure until we talk to Corrine, but it certainly seems that way."

Arryn shook her head. "Somehow, all I got out of that was that you can't come up with a good nickname to save your life." She reached over and scratched the rabbit between the ears. "I'm sorry, Fuzzy Lumpkins von Poofbottom You'll have to forgive him. He doesn't have many brain cells left."

The rabbit's ears perked up a second before the tigers' did, and Arryn immediately went on alert. She reached out with her nature magic first out of instinct, searching for life.

On the water, she sensed several presences.

"There are people approaching in the water," she reported.

Lorelei turned toward the water, her eyes glowing aqua. "I'll check it out."

"You shouldn't go alone," Arryn cautioned.

Lorelei smiled. "In the water, no one can touch me. Had our cousins stayed in the water instead of heading to land, they would've survived."

Cathillian nodded. "We can understand. The forest is where we are most deadly."

The Daoine woman wasted no more time before running and jumping into the water. Arryn could feel the swell of power around Lorelei just before she dove under the surface, propelling herself out to sea.

"Damn," she said. "They really are fast in the water."

Cathillian nodded. "We're not even that fast in the forest. We'd have to learn how to fly."

Bast laughed. "Or just learn how to properly use your legs. But I know how much you forest people *love* physical magic." She rolled her eyes.

"Hey, I would love to learn how to use physical magic to kick and punch harder, run faster, and build walls that will keep assholes off our land. Unfortunately, I have a mother who is very scary, and I don't think she would like it," Cathillian said.

Arryn nodded. "Yeah. What he said. His mommy wouldn't like it." She laughed, then promptly hissed when Cathillian lightly punched her in the shoulder. "*Ouch*, you dick."

A mischievous smile spread across Bast's lips. "Want me to punch him back for you?"

The same devious smile spread on Arryn's face. "I think that would be a wonderful idea."

"Hey, hey, hey!" Cathillian said, backing away with his hands in the air. "Now, now, ladies. No need to be feisty."

"You're lucky you're cute," Bast said. "Otherwise, I have a feeling she'd have killed you by now."

Arryn nodded. "You know, I'm starting to think that really is the only thing that has saved him over the years. And not just from me."

Cathillian laughed. "I'm pretty sure you're not wrong."

Arryn, Cathillian, and Bast each picked a direction and watched closely for anyone approaching. Bast monitored any vibrations in the ground, while Cathillian used nature magic to search for life. Arryn, on the other hand, decided to practice her mental magic.

She opened her mind, wincing at the almost immediate headache that accompanied it. Mystical magic certainly didn't come easy for her. One-on-one telepathy didn't cause any major issues, and meditation was a breeze—but attempting to stay connected to more than one mind at a time, or using telepathy across significant distances, or opening her mind to sense the consciousness of others seemed to bring on headaches.

But that couldn't stop her. She had to find a way to get past it.

Only ten minutes had passed before Lorelei returned with a small boat following behind her. She had used her magic to propel the craft through the water.

"I'm assuming that's a sign that they're not terrible people?" Bast said.

Lorelei stood, walking out of the water toward them. "This is an interesting development."

"What is it? Who are they?" Arryn asked.

Lorelei turned her head to look over her shoulder as a small group of people were already pulling a boat into the sand and turning to walk toward Arryn and the others. "They're Storm Callers."

Arryn looked at her curiously. "Aren't they the ones causing all the problems?"

Lorelei shook her head. "They are different. In fact, they stopped at Brann's village; they saw the smoke and knew what happened, because they're hunting the Raider ship. When I saw them rowing this way, I went out to question them. They brought all the village's survivors onboard to care for them. I went to the ship and verified it myself; they were all safe, below deck."

"That's great news!" Arryn said.

"As soon as we finish here, I'm going to escort the Caller and her crew back to their ship, and then get my cousins into the water. I'll take them back to our home, where they will be safe. Brann will be so happy. This is wonderful news; now we have help."

"Hello. My name is Mariana. This is Captain Veren. I hear we might be after the same people. We would like to help."

CHAPTER TWENTY

Mariana's information turned out to be quite helpful. The idea was to find out all they could before attacking; Arryn's plan had been to sneak up on the encampment and spy inside. But she had no idea what it looked like, how many guards there were—if any—or how strong their forces might be. Though she'd learned that the Raiders were training others in their camp.

Because of the exploration of Mariana's crewmate, Smiley, Arryn narrowly avoided walking into what could have been a disastrous situation. Smiley led them to the part of the mountain he had easily climbed. It was rocky, but there was a clear-cut path leading up to a small ledge.

They walked carefully along the ledge, which was no more than five feet wide, until they saw the outline of the encampment. They dropped down and began to crawl.

"This kinda fucking sucks, Smiley," Captain Veren grumbled quietly.

"Do you have a better plan to keep from being seen?" Smiley retorted.

"Everyone shut up. We're getting close enough that someone

might hear," Arryn said as quietly but as authoritatively as she could manage.

They crawled fifty more feet, and Arryn felt a tug at her ankle. She looked back to see Bast staring at her, eyes blue. Bast pointed up toward the top of the mountain and moved her finger in a circle, signaling there were several people around.

Risking the headache, Arryn quickly went through her group's roster and sent a silent *'Stop'* to each. She felt Smiley, Veren, Mariana, Bast, and Lorelei all quickly follow her order.

Moving from one person to the next hadn't been any less painful than communicating to everyone at once. That was something to file away for later.

Arryn reached out with her nature magic, feeling for whoever or whatever might be approaching. She was met with seven life forms only twenty feet above them, every one of them human.

Shit, she thought to herself. Then she took a deep breath and told everyone at once, *There are several people on the ledge above us. Stay quiet.*

They weren't far from the encampment, and Arryn wondered if they were part of it, or just some random wanderers. Judging how close they were, her gut told her it was the former—the worst-case scenario.

Arryn heard arguing above, but couldn't understand anything until one of the participants got close.

"You almost made me drop this damn thing right off the edge! Quit fucking around. That bitch could be anywhere."

Arryn smiled, wondering if the bitch they spoke of was her. *That's quite a compliment, thank you. I'll take it,* she smiled to herself.

"Hey! Who the fuck are you?" the same voice demanded from above.

"Uh oh," she said, peering up. "Well, subtlety's no longer an option."

"Move! Now!" the man above her shouted to the other people in attendance.

Arryn felt three distinct explosions of magic—the very same type of magic used when teleporting—and five of the seven people disappeared.

Everyone in her group scrambled to their feet, the tigers roaring as they began scaling the wall. Alarms began to sound in the distance, and Arryn turned to see the gates opening, releasing dozens of armed men.

A familiar *click* sounded, and she looked up in time to see the man pulling back a crossbow bolt, his gaze locked on the tigers now approaching him. Arryn's eyes flashed black, and she reached up with her arm, wrapping her telekinetic energy around him, and pulled as hard as she could. The man flew over them, off the side of the mountain, and down to his sandy grave below.

Pain ripped through her shoulder, and she heard a pain-filled cry come from above. Dante had been hit. It wasn't fatal, unlike the head-crushing chomp he took out of the man who shot him.

"Arryn, there are at least fifty of them, and they have magitech weapons," Cathillian reasoned.

"We might be able to take the ones coming for us now, but not the flood that will follow," Bast added. "We have to go. Now."

Arryn almost growled. "Fuck. Fine. Let's go."

Bast nodded. "But first…"

Her eyes flashed blue again as she looked down at the approaching men. Some of them had stopped and were loading crossbows. She lifted her hands, her fingers dancing, and the sand below began to shift and move.

Straightening her wrists, lifting her hands even higher, she erected a wall of sand. She then thrust her hands forward, shooting the grains of the wall toward the men, blinding them. Their screams erupted from below as they fought the sand, trying to wipe it away from their eyes but only making it worse.

Bast turned to Arryn. "There, that should buy some time. You should see the sandstorms Cleo and I can make together. *Huge.*"

Arryn just shook her head in awe.

"We should take to the trees," Cathillian decided. "I hear the sounds of horses coming from inside the encampment; I think they are preparing for a larger assault."

Arryn nodded. "We don't want to lead them to the Daoine. We need to go a different path."

She wasn't nearly as agile in the trees as Corrine was, especially with other people in tow, but it would still be faster than running on foot, and their pursuers wouldn't be able to see which direction they went.

Arryn and Cathillian's eyes flashed green, and their hands reached up, causing trees high on the ledge to drop vines. The two druids wrapped each person in their party in a sort of harness to make it easier to pull them into the trees. Then Arryn sent a quick message to Snow and Dante to climb.

Though Dante was injured, he managed to get up onto a thick, low branch. Arryn went to him, quickly pulled the dart free, and healed him. "Stay in the trees and move as quickly as possible."

The tiger cub nuzzled her for a brief moment before climbing higher into the tree and leaping onto the next.

Cathillian and Arryn worked together to call new vines, pulling their friends from one tree to the next until they reached the location they had met Mariana.

"Lorelei, we're going to lower you, Mariana, Smiley, and the captain. Get them out to their ship as fast as possible, and get your people to safety. Mariana, you need to get your ship around the other side of the cove. Keep it out of sight. The Raiders know we're here, but they don't know that you are—*yet.* Let's keep it that way," Arryn said.

Everyone nodded in understanding. Arryn and Cathillian lowered the trio down to the beach, making sure they made it to the boat with the other men and back onto the water before continuing on themselves. Arryn had sensed Snow and Dante moving along through the trees, and knew she and Cathillian weren't far behind.

By the time they made it back to the slide, Lorelei had returned with what was left of her family from Brann's village. She had taken straight to the water and had used her power to propel her quickly to the storm ship.

Arryn and the others went down the slide, careful to tuck their arms in, and ran toward the beach.

"That was a little closer than I would like to admit," Arryn noted as Lorelei approached the edge of the water.

Lorelei nodded. "Yes, it was. But you managed to save us. I think you should come with me now; it seems your friends have already been allowed inside."

"It's a long swim, and I'm sure it's very scary for land dwellers, but I promise nothing will happen to you," Lorelei assured them.

Arryn nodded and smiled. "Lead the way."

Arryn trudged into the water after Lorelei and stepped off the deep drop. Cathillian and Bast followed close behind.

CHAPTER TWENTY-ONE

Esmerelda stood, seething at the three men before her. On the floor was a mother and child they had managed to take from a meaningless tribe of water people down the coast.

Her nostrils flared as she crossed her arms over her chest and stared daggers into the men standing but a few feet away. "Let me get this straight. You went there… Took these two *things*… And on your way back, saw the *one* person we need to kill, and thought to yourself, 'I should just let her go'?"

One of the men shook his head. "No. Gabe told us to go, so we did. He thought getting them back here and telling you what was happening was more important. If we had all died confronting the druid, you wouldn't have known she had found our camp until it was too late."

Esmerelda sighed, angrily clicking her teeth together. "Explain to me again why you thought I would want two freakish water peasants."

The three men anxiously looked at one another before a different one addressed her. "You remember the story the Raiders told when they came? They raided that Daoine village and killed all those people? Well, Selena said she believes the ship that was after them is still following them. So, we offered to head down the beach to search for it."

Her eyes closed. "And *who* told you to do that? *I* am your leader. *Not* Selena."

"We're sorry. We thought if the ship really was coming for them, that they would find them here with us, and then all of us would be in danger."

"And them?" Esmerelda asked, gesturing to the mother and child who were holding each other on the floor.

"We went all the way to the end of the beach and found a group of people playing on this weird spiral thing made out of glass. There was a rearick, a woman with magic I can't even begin to explain, and a little girl who looked like a druid. From the story we heard from the few who returned from the Heights, it seemed like they were part of Arryn's group. We lost four of our men but managed to grab these two." He clasped his hands, repeatedly twiddling his fingers in anxiety.

Esmerelda paced back and forth. They had found half the group, which meant Arryn had left the warriors to protect the Daoine. That meant the tribe was of importance to the woman.

"There's more," one of the men said.

She turned cold eyes on him. "What?"

He cleared his throat. "On the way down, we didn't see anything. But on the way back, there was a beached dinghy, and several men sitting beside it. They were dressed and armed quite like the Raiders; I believe that dinghy belonged to the enemy ship."

She sighed and growled. "So, they're here, too. *Fucking fantastic.*"

"What would you have us do?" he asked.

There was a moment of silence as she thought it over. She looked at the terrified mother clutching her child and rolled her eyes. "Well, it seems the lot of you brought her down on us with your stupidity. So now we have to improvise. Use the two of them to send a message."

The men looked at one another before turning back to her. "What kind of message?"

She gave a dark smile. "The type of message my dearly departed husband would have sent. Use your imagination. Then bring Selena to me; she and I need to make plans."

***

Arryn looked around the cave, amazed at what the Daoine people had created. They had built an entire home inside of the mountain. It had started out as only a tiny hole, a cave under the water only large enough to house a single person.

From there, they had burrowed deeper and created a beautiful living space. She was fascinated by these people and what they were capable of. She couldn't wait until everything was over, and she could talk to Brann more about his relationship with Finn.

Unfortunately, things were going to get far worse before they started to get better.

While Arryn was away with Lorelei and the others, there had been an attack. Samuel, Cleo, and even Corrine had fought bravely to protect the Daoine people, but physical magic proved to be too much for the peaceful water dwellers. Arryn's friends had to choose between saving everyone and fleeing to safety, or staying to fight, and potentially dying; if they fought and died, the Daoine people would surely fall shortly after.

Sam, Cleo, and Corrine had made the right call, but two people—a mother and child—had still been taken.

Arryn paced back and forth, shaking her hands vigorously as she tried to calm herself. "They were right there. *Right* there! I could've saved them."

Cathillian grabbed Arryn by the shoulders. "Stop pacing. You said it yourself: they were teleported out. There was no way for you to know who was with them or where they went."

She looked at him with rage. "I should've assumed! Five people disappeared, but there were only three blasts of magic."

"Arryn… I love you, and I love your dedication to people and your sense of duty. But you're *reaching*. This was not your fault. You know as well as I do that not all Arcadians know how to teleport. Only the strongest. Why on Irth would you have imagined it was five guards and two hostages, instead of three men who could teleport and four who couldn't?"

She stared up into his eyes, seeing his concern for her. She sighed as she closed her eyes. "You're right. It just… They were right there."

Cathillian pulled her into a hug, but it was brief, as the tigers —who were outside of the cave, on top of the mountain—began to roar. Echo called out right behind them. Arryn quickly pulled back, reaching through the bond as she did. Her eyes flashed green as she looked through Snow's eyes. Cathillian did the same with Echo.

The tiger could smell blood off in the distance, and see a shadow approaching on the beach in the moonlit night.

Arryn pulled back, gasping. "There is someone coming, and they're hurt."

Lorelei quickly made her way over. "I'll take you up."

"We all go this time, lass," Samuel said. "Not that I'm a fan of bein' underwater that long."

Arryn gave a quick smile and clapped Samuel on the back before following Lorelei to the edge of the water. One after another, they all dove in, and the Daoine woman encompassed each of their heads in a small air bubble.

While Arryn was good enough at propelling herself through the water, like Corrine in the trees, she knew Lorelei and the other Elders would be much faster.

They reached the edge of the beach in no time at all, and

Arryn quickly jumped out, rushing forward. She had no weapons, but she was ready for confrontation, should one arise.

Something heavy hit the sand behind her, and she looked back to see Snow and Dante land only a few feet apart. They followed her as she slowly approached the figure in the darkness.

Arryn took a deep breath, her eyes clouding over as she reached for the mind that was getting closer—then she cried out, falling to her knees as she clutched her side.

Cathillian rushed over, kneeled beside her, and brushed her hair back. "Are you okay? What happened?"

Arryn shook her head. "It's not me. It's her." She pointed at the oncoming figure and pulled back on the mystical magic, needing to break away from the woman's mind and the intense pain that she felt.

Alongside all the physical agony was an intense heartbreak Arryn couldn't even begin to imagine. It was so overwhelming that Arryn wasn't even able to make out what was wrong.

She climbed to her feet and began to run, everyone else following close behind. As she drew closer, her eyes widened, and chills ran through her body as she realized what she was seeing.

The silhouette quickly revealed itself to be a woman carrying a child. Each step was slow and deliberate, but they were also staggered and seemingly painful. From what Arryn had felt not moments before, she knew the pain to be true.

Arryn ran as hard as she could, afraid to teleport and scare the mother. As she reached the pair, the moonlight revealed blood-stained clothes, both the mother's and the child's.

Tears began to stream down Arryn's face. She felt for life, but only found a single spark between the two figures. She looked into the woman's eyes, which were bloodshot and filled with tears of her own.

Arryn jerked as the woman spoke.

"She's gone. They said this was a message for you."

Unbelievable guilt, hatred, rage, and a plethora of other emotions washed over Arryn as she realized that the men who had taken the mother and child had recognized Arryn and told Esmerelda of her presence.

The woman began to fall, and Arryn reached out to catch her and her lifeless child, carefully lowering both to the ground.

"I can heal you," Arryn offered, fighting her voice to respond through the tears.

The woman shook her head. "She was all I had. Just let me go with her."

Arryn quickly assessed the woman's wounds, using her magic, but it only took a second to discover they were not fatal. They would take a very long time to heal, and she would feel the pain of the process, but she would survive.

"Your wounds are bad, but not bad enough to take you," Arryn said gently.

"Please, let her heal you," Lorelei added as she knelt next to the woman.

The woman groaned as she shifted her daughter in her arms. Arryn tried to help, but the mother simply shook her head, welcoming the struggle of laying her daughter comfortably next to her in her arms.

"Let me be with her. I don't care what you have to do."

Arryn looked to the sky and took a deep breath, doing everything she could to will the tears to stop. She looked back down and laid her hand on the mother's shoulder. "I'm so sorry. I came here to save lives. I never meant—"

The mother shook her head again, interrupting Arryn. "They meant for this to be a message for you, but that doesn't mean this is your fault. We were the casualties, but your friends fought bravely to save us. If you want to make this right, save them. Let no one else suffer what I just had to."

Arryn's brows furrowed as she leaned forward and placed a

gentle hand on the woman's forehead. "I swear to you… I *will* make them pay for this."

The woman nodded. "Now let me go. Let me be with my little girl and her daddy. Don't let me hold you back from your fight any longer. If you don't strike first, they will."

Arryn looked away for a moment, her eyes searching for Cathillian. She didn't have to look far—he was there, kneeling next to her. He nodded, and she turned back to the grieving mother.

The Elders began to gather around the three women, their horror, grief, and rage palpable in the night air.

"Your family is here with you," Arryn assured her, taking another deep breath.

The woman nodded. "Good. Then they will all know I chose this."

"You will feel no pain," Arryn promised, securing one hand on the woman's forehead as she placed the other between her and her daughter, just over the woman's heart. "You'll be with her soon."

The woman leaned forward and kissed her daughter on the forehead, and then Arryn began.

Her eyes flashed green as she focused her energy on the woman's life force, pulling what was left from her body. It was slow at first, and the mother became tired. Arryn could feel her drifting off to sleep, just before she accelerated the process.

As promised, the mother felt no pain. As she took her final breath, and her heart beat for the last time, Arryn felt a part of her own humanity slip.

All the rage and sorrow in the world settled on her shoulders; she had never before had to end the life of an innocent. As she looked at the mother and child, an array of thoughts and emotions hit her all at once.

In the child, she somehow saw Corrine, and the weight of that loss destroyed Arryn on a level she had never imagined. She may not have given birth to Corrine, but she certainly understood why the mother had made the decision to die with her child—she couldn't imagine living in a world without her.

Arryn pulled her hands away, both of them shaking uncontrollably, with thoughts of vengeance running rampant in her mind.

"Arryn," Cathillian cautioned.

She could hear the warning in his voice, just as she had heard it the day of her trials. It hadn't registered with her then, and it wasn't going to now. Just like the *Versuch*, she felt herself losing control.

She stood as thunder clapped loudly overhead, and lightning webbed through a sky of clouds that had only just begun to form. Tears streamed down her face as chills ripped through her body.

"*Arryn!*"

She heard Corrine call her name, but in that moment, it didn't matter; no one but the Bitch herself could keep her from what she had planned.

Her hate-filled black and green eyes looked pointedly over at Snow and Dante, only a flash of emotion ringing out through the bond between them. The tigress didn't hesitate to get to her feet and rush over, while Dante momentarily disappeared back up the mountain.

"What is she doing?" Lorelei asked, her voice frantic. "Is she okay? What's happening?"

Arryn mounted Snow and looked over at her worried friends, Lorelei's concerned face among them. "I made a promise to her, and I'm going to keep it."

"Arryn, you need to wait for us." Cathillian's voice was forceful and deadly serious.

She shook her head. "I need to do this alone. Right now, I can't think of anyone else. They did this to send a fucking message? Well, I have one for *them*."

Dante rushed up, her pack gripped in his large jaws. He

flinched as thunder shook the ground. She pulled the quiver free from his grip, then detached the bow. Both were placed diagonally across her back before she nodded to Dante, who kept the bag in his jaws.

Arryn flexed her legs as she squeezed Snow's side to let her know she was ready.

As the tiger lurched forward, a lightning bolt ripped from the sky and struck a tree on the ledge of the mountain above. The thick trunk snapped and tumbled down to the sandy beach, only fifty feet away.

Arryn took another deep breath; she hadn't meant to do that, and if she didn't get herself under control, she would bring her own death before justice was served.

CHAPTER TWENTY-TWO

Arryn's eyes flashed white as she went into a light trance, meditating to recover as much energy as possible. She would need all the help she could get once she reached the encampment.

The trip had been a long one for the tigers, but it had gone by in a flash for her, as she had been lost in her mind for nearly all of it.

Snow sent a brief flash of anticipation through the bond, pulling Arryn out of her meditative state. She saw they were closing in on the wall. On top, she could make out eight silhouettes—twice as many as before.

Removing the bow, she pulled an arrow free from the quiver, nocked it, and aimed at the guard farthest to the left. She shot, rapidly nocking another and aiming for the guard all the way to the right.

The guards were surrounded by torchlight, while the clouds Arryn had created covered the moon and shrouded her in darkness. They were illuminated, easily visible while they scurried about trying to find her, while she picked them off one at a time.

The last guard managed to load a crossbow and aim it directly at her. The moment his eyes found her, she loosed, the arrow piercing his throat and sending him tumbling over her side of the wall.

Snow skidded to a stop, and Arryn slid off. Dante was just behind; each of the animals expectantly awaited their orders.

"This will be dangerous; they'll have magitech weapons. Stay out here," she commanded.

She started to go, then turned back. "But I know the two of you… If you do go inside, stick to the shadows. Snow, remember Arcadia. Be smart."

Wasting no more time, Arryn ran toward the outside wall that faced the ocean. She rounded the corner and opened her senses. She could feel people moving around, but it seemed no one was aware yet of what she had done.

It had been a risk, but she knew the alarm that had been set earlier had been from inside, not from the men on the wall. The fact that everything was still quiet proved her theory correct.

Once she reached the halfway point, she once again threw the bow over her shoulder. She placed her hands flat against the wall, feeling for plant life on the other side. Sand wasn't exactly something she was used to, and she didn't feel that it would be an easy feat to conjure a vine.

The edges of the inside wall were lined with raised boxes filled with soil. Each box contained a different plant: tomatoes, cucumbers, berries, watermelon.

Her eyes flashed green as she focused on the watermelon vines, thickening them as they traveled over the wall. She grabbed hold of one and placed her feet against the stone.

When she reached the top, she placed her hands on the ledge and searched for nearby life. She felt no humans in the immediate area, so she quickly pulled herself over and lowered her body into the plant bed.

Ducking down, she looked around at the immediate area. She was surrounded by tents, but they were over ten feet away—far enough that sun would easily reach the plants during the daylight hours.

Jumping down onto the sand, Arryn stayed low as she ran to the first tent to her right. She crept up behind it and sensed two life forms inside. Pulling the knife from the sheath on her hip, she jabbed it into the fabric near the ground. The quiet cutting was completely drowned out by the ambient sounds of fires and passersby.

Ducking down again, she slid inside the hole she'd made.

"Yes, I think she will," a man said.

His female companion laughed. "That was a bold move on Esmerelda's part, but I think it will scare them, all the same. Some think it will only make things worse, but I think those disgusting people will retreat to whatever hole they hide in."

"Meh… I wouldn't bet on that last bit," Arryn said as she stood. Both speakers turned to face her, their eyes wide. "That 'only making things worse' bit, though? Oh yeah. *Much* worse."

The woman opened her mouth to scream, and Arryn's eyes flashed black, as her left hand reached out and gave a twist.

The woman's head spun to the side, a sickening crack echoing inside the tent.

Her companion turned hateful eyes on Arryn, but before he could even take the first step, the blade in Arryn's right hand was buried in his chest.

She crossed the tent quickly, pulling the other blade from her left sheath before jabbing it upward under his chin. She silently lowered him to the ground and removed both blades from his body. After cleaning them off using his shirt, she made her way out the back of the tent, and moved onto the next one.

This tent only held one single man, who had apparently gotten drunk and passed out early. She could smell the scent of blood permeating the air as soon as she cut the tent wall open. When she made her way inside, she found his clothing lying beside the bed, soaked in blood, and she knew it belonged to the mother and child she had so recently laid to rest.

She stalked over to the bed and leaned over, placing a hand over his mouth. The man's eyes opened just as her knife touched his throat. "I got your fucking message. And now, you're part of the message I have for Esmerelda," she said, her voice barely above a whisper.

His hand made to grab for her, but she slit his throat, stopping it midair. His body flinched and kicked as he fought against his death, but she fought back and kept her hand clamped over his mouth until the bitter end.

Then Arryn made her way to the next tent. She managed to kill two of the three men inside, but the last one proved to be quite the opponent. As she rushed for him, he ducked out of the way and kicked her in the stomach. She fell to her knees, and he kicked her hard in the side.

She rolled onto her back as he jumped down on top of her, pinning her hands down to the ground. He smiled as he wedged his knee between her legs. "Nice of you to come to visit," he said.

She smiled in return. "Thanks for having me. But I don't think I'll be staying for long."

He thrust his head forward, crushing her nose. She groaned loudly, but bit down hard, grinding her teeth to keep her from crying out.

He placed both of her wrists in one hand. She'd wanted to get out without a sound, and continue making her rounds around the camp, but it didn't seem like that was going to be an option.

Fuck, she thought. *If I'd been practicing mental magic this whole time, I might have been able to pull an illusion out of my ass. At the very least, I could've knocked his ass out.*

He thrust his head forward again as she kneed him in the side, and the sound of her nose now breaking echoed in her mind, disorienting her again. The next thing she knew, the sounds of shots from a magitech rifle and shouting were ringing through her ears.

Shit. Plan B, it is.

Arryn twisted her fingers, and the blades on either side flew through the air to stab her target through each temple. As he fell on top of her, she quickly reached up, grabbed the ram's horn handles of her weapons, and pulled them free.

She pressed her fingers to the bridge of her nose, giving a rough jerk to push the bones back together. Heat filled her face as the broken pieces began to heal, allowing her the ability to focus again.

Loud footsteps quickly approached, and her eyes flashed black. Her magic swelled around her before imploding, teleporting her out of that tent and into the next.

Inside, she was met by two men quickly climbing out of separate beds to get dressed. Without saying a word, Arryn rushed toward the one on her right. She shoved her foot down on the side of his knee, then pushed her knee upward into his face as he stumbled forward.

The man behind her punched her in the face as she turned. She fell back a few steps, then dove forward, ramming her shoulder into his abdomen and tackling him onto his bed. She kneed him in the groin, then lifted him up and headbutted him in the face.

As she ran her knife under his chin, she heard a large pack of dogs growling and barking outside. The animals sounded vicious, and she could feel their intense need to impress their screaming masters.

As Arryn stood and wiped her blade off on the man's only partially pulled-up pants, she smiled. "Oh, that was not wise of them."

As the first dog burst through the open flap of the tent, her eyes flashed green and her hand shot forward. The dog was immediately overcome with a sense of tranquility.

"I am not your enemy," she said softly enough for the dog to hear, but no one else. Her hand moved to point toward the door. "They are."

The dog lowered his head as he backed out of the tent, and she immediately heard a man scream, as the dog attacked his cruel master.

These people were not nature magic users, so Arryn knew these dogs had to have been trained by force. Beaten. Mistreated. Tortured. That was how they were trained to obey, how they were trained to kill.

These dogs would get their revenge today, as well.

Arryn heard a large crowd closing in on her as men and women barked orders at dogs and guards. Then the unmistakable sound of two tigers roaring into the night sky descended upon the camp like a death call. Arryn closed her eyes, focusing on her familiars.

Dante took one side of the camp, while Snow took the other. They took turns intimidating the attack dogs and the shouting people before returning to the shadows. They never walked out past the outermost line of tents, making them more elusive and terrifying.

Through what little mental magic she was able to touch—especially without risking the headache—she could feel the uncertainty and fear rising among the people.

That was exactly what she wanted; she wanted them to feel intense fear. She wanted them to know exactly what was coming for them, as payment for what they had done.

Just as the crowd began to descend on the tent she was in, she once again allowed her magic to swell around her. In a flash, she teleported from the tent to near the largest fire in the center of the encampment.

People rushing through the area immediately stopped and turned toward her.

She smiled. "Is all this for little ol' me? Aw, ya shouldn't have."

"Attack!" one of the guards shouted, sending a rush of dogs running straight for her, growling and jaws snapping.

She flexed her entire body, and a barrier exploded around her, knocking back several approaching guards. Green began to bleed into the blackness of her eyes as she focused on the wall of dogs coming at her.

She threw her hands out, and the dogs slowly came to a stop. The growling became quieter, and then stopped altogether as she continued to push her influence on them. The effect was slow and steady—not overwhelming and overpowering, like the magic the dark druids had used.

"What the fuck?" one of the guards in the crowd said. "*Attack!*"

A dark smile formed on Arryn's face. "You heard the man. *Attack.*"

The dogs immediately dispersed, growling and snapping as they rushed into the crowd of people. Everyone screamed and rushed around, trying to avoid being bitten.

Another roar, quickly followed by another, completely swallowed the other sounds, as the tigers jumped into the middle of the crowd where Arryn was. She opened her barrier just enough to allow the tigers to rush inside, expanding it enough to cloak them, as well.

Fireballs began to rain down on her, but the shield protected her and the tigers. She looked to her left to see that Dante still had her bag. She reached inside and pulled out a box, carefully opening it with telekinetic magic. She used that same magic to lift another box from the bag; the only two mines she had.

She levitated both mines out of their respective boxes, well aware she only had enough magic left to get them free.

She couldn't afford anything else. The sounds of fireballs hitting the shield brought her attention back to the crowd, and she saw several men now aiming magitech rifles at her. Her shield was more than enough to deflect the magitech rifle blasts, but not while also deflecting fireballs and levitating mines.

Drop down, she sent to her familiars.

They quickly followed her orders, and then she used the very shallow bond she had with the dogs to send them fleeing from the camp to safety. She had a feeling the front gate was wide open now, with people trying to flee for their lives.

She took a deep breath and smiled as she addressed everyone in the immediate area. "We'll be waiting for you. And if you think *I'm* bad, there's *far* worse forces waiting for me to return."

She dropped her shield and spun, telekinetic energy bursting from her body to deflect everything coming for her, and also slinging the mines into the approaching guards and Raiders.

She quickly placed her hands on both of her tigers, her eyes flashing completely black as her magic wrapped around all three of them. In a large implosion of magic, the force fueled by her fear, the three of them were teleported out of the camp and nearly halfway to the Daoine village.

She hadn't meant to put so much force into it, but the brief flash of fear she had felt forced her to put everything she had left into the magic.

THE LANDING WAS NOT GENTLE. As her magic spat them out on the other side, Arryn lost consciousness and hit the ground hard, breaking her arm before rolling to a rough stop in the sand. The tigers hit just as hard, but their large, muscled bodies took the fall much better.The tigers quickly recoiled and jumped to their feet, rushing over to Arryn.

Snow nudged her, first with a large paw, and then with her warm nose. Neither one seemed to work. She laid down on the ground, grumbling at her cub. Dante quickly grabbed Arryn's feet in his mouth and dragged her body over Snow's back.

Once she was secure—as secure as she could be—Snow stood and began trekking back toward the Daoine village.

They hadn't traveled far before Snow heard rustling in the trees, high on the edge of the mountain. She felt a calm wash over her and sensed Cathillian's magic. She stopped running as she and Dante waited for the druid to approach.

Arryn stirred on Snow's back, and the tiger heard the distinct sound of bone breaking. She could feel the heat emanating from Arryn's body, and she realized someone was healing her. Snow carefully laid back down in the sand as her passenger began to come around.

Two bright, neon green orbs glowed as they approached from the darkness. The eyes of young Corrine. Her arms were outstretched, and even Snow could sense the magic emanating from her tiny body.

Arryn groaned as she slid off Snow. The tiger turned just enough to look at her, and licked her face as she came to.

As the young woman began to sit up on the ground, the tiger blew out a loud *huff* of relief, and then flopped her head down on Arryn's feet to rest.

CHAPTER TWENTY-THREE

Esmerelda stood in the middle of the camp; the fires were barely smoldering as the sun began to peek over the horizon. Her arms were crossed over her chest, her teeth nearly breaking from how tightly her jaws were clamped, and her nostrils flared as her female guards stood around her. She stared at the heap of bodies next to the largest fire pit in the center of camp.

"Thirty. One girl took out thirty of our men and women. How? How is this possible?" Esmerelda asked no one in particular. "When I heard that number, I thought several druids had broken in here. I mean, seriously. That's impossible, right?" Her voice began to rise as her irritation grew. "It's impossible that a *single* girl could do the work of *a dozen fucking men!*"

Her personal guard stood taller, preparing to carry out any orders she might give, but the men in the area shrank back a little.

"I want her dead. I don't *just* want her dead… I want it to be painful. Torturous. I want her fucking *ancestors* to feel it. We know where those sea beasts live now. We know where that bitch fled to. It stands to reason the other storm ship is down there, too. Everyone we want dead, all in one place. So convenient."

"We can't just go charging in blind. You heard what she said last night—there are more of her. If we're worried about *her*, why the hell would we charge in without knowing who *else* is with her?" Captain Seth asked.

Esmerelda turned, cocking her head to the side as she smiled. "Well, Captain. I suppose that's why it's a good thing this has nothing to do with you. You've been relieved of your duty."

His brows furrowed as anger etched across his face. "What the hell did you just say?"

Esmerelda rolled her eyes as she waved a hand. Selena came to stand by her side, a dark smile on her face. "I said, you are relieved of duty. You are nothing but useless scum. Selena will take your place; she's the one with all the power on the ship, anyway. You are just a novelty. A title," Esmerelda said with ice dripping from her voice.

"You will *not* take my ship from me. If you think for an instant the men will follow y—"

Captain Seth's head was violently relieved of his body by a man loyal to Selena.

"Unfortunately, Captain Seth is no longer available to work with us," Esmerelda said with an almost seductive smile. "I'm going to allow Selena to take it from here. If I stare at this pile of bodies any longer, I'm going to have all of you slaughtered."

Esmerelda gave Selena a curt nod, and the new captain stepped forward to address the crowd. "She snuck up on us last night, but that was a terrible mistake. Her actions here have only angered us and made us stronger. Consequently, her actions have made *her* weaker. All magic users suffer fatigue, and you can bet your ass she's feeling the effects today.

"We may be down thirty men, but we have a couple hundred more—most of whom use magic—not to mention the magitech weapons. She has an army of pacifist ocean dwellers. Even with the Storm Callers on their side, their numbers are nothing to speak of. Our time is *now*! Let's move and attack them directly!"

One of the men stepped forward, obvious concern on his face. "And what if they take to the water? They are water dwellers, after all. And you know as well as I do the storm crew is best in the water, too."

Selena smiled. "But I'm *better*. The ocean will bend to *me*, and it will become their grave. Follow me, and we will have victory. And with Esmerelda, we will have the weapons to make sure no one can ever stand in our way; the world will be ours for the taking."

There was a moment of hesitation before cheers erupted and fists rose into the air. Esmerelda sat back, a smile on her face as she felt the excited nervousness rising in her belly, felt the electric tingle of power in the air. She suddenly understood why her late husband loved going to war.

SLOWLY, Arryn's eyes fluttered open. Only a bit of light shone in through the air vents built into the walls of the mountain. She squinted her eyes as she rolled over to her side, realizing she was lying directly in one of the rays.

As she sat up, flashes of the night before began to return to her. Faces of the men whose lives she had taken popped into her mind, but then vanished as the faces of the innocent mother and child came back. She ran through the entire night's events, wondering if she had possibly gone too far.

But then a familiar anger settled in her belly.

Those men had killed people. In the Heights. On the road to Arcadia. In villages and on farms. They had stolen cattle, money, and only the Bitch knew what else. Some of those men had even been in the forest and had fought alongside Jerick and Alaric—only having survived because they had fled the fight.

The Storm Raiders, too, had killed indiscriminately up and down the coast, taking the lives of Brann's family in the other Daoine village. They came to the Farriage Coast for no other reason than to find weapons that would allow them to kill even more people, take more things, and ruin more lives.

And now both groups were working together.

No… she hadn't gone *too* far. She hadn't gone *far enough*. They had to be stopped before any more children, mothers, fathers, brothers, or sisters died for nothing.

"I know that look," Cathillian said as he walked over.

Arryn looked around, aware for the first time that the cave was full of people. Not only the Daoine; the Storm Callers had been invited inside, as well.

A lot must have happened while I was asleep.

"Yeah, I know you do," she said, responding to his remark.

"You scared the hell out of us," he said. All she could do was nod in return. "I don't think you realize just how bad it was. I saw you burst through an explosion of magic, and I thought you landed terribly. It wasn't until I read Snow's thoughts…"

She nodded again. "I know."

He sighed and crouched down, taking her hand in his and kissing the back of it before pressing it to his cheek. His eyes closed as his brows furrowed. After a moment, he sat, still holding her hand.

"I suppose you'd like an update?" he asked.

She smiled softly. "It's funny that even when I go off the deep end, you just warn me about the dangers and let it go. You never yell at me."

"Would it be effective?" he asked with amusement in his voice. She shook her head and smiled even brighter. He laughed and said, "It wouldn't do any good, and I have no reason to make you hate me. The way I see it, if I piss you off, you're likely to do something even more reckless."

"I don't know why I'm so stubborn, but I'm glad you know me

as well as you do." She sighed and once again looked around the cave. "How about that update?"

He nodded. "When we found you, your arm was broken in two places, and you had two cracked ribs. You are lucky you didn't break your neck. We rushed you back to the cave and brought you inside so Corrine and Brann could heal you, but you remained unconscious."

Arryn's brows lifted in surprise. "Brann healed me, too?"

Cathillian smiled. "You would be proud of Corrine. She has been glued to Brann's side, teaching him how to embrace his healing talent; she even taught him how to call vines. Well, they had to use seaweed, but it worked the same. If he's ever in the forest, he will be able to do the spell."

At that moment, Arryn felt so much pride. "That's amazing. It's incredible to think just how far she's come in such a short time."

He nodded. "It really is. Brann also introduced us to Finn. Interesting story... We can't talk to the sea mammals—at all. Brann can, though. Well, *kind* of. I don't think it's a power that was taught, like the founder taught my grandfather. I think this is just an evolution in their magic."

"That's crazy. I can't imagine our magic evolving again. Can you? I mean, what the hell else would we be able to accomplish?" she said with wonder.

Cathillian shrugged. "I don't know about that. Corrine worked with Brann on talking to the dolphin, though. While she was unable to directly show him how to communicate with Finn, she said she was able to teach him what you taught her. He was a quick study. Picked it right up."

Arryn smiled. "I'm so proud of her. She's eight; think of what she'll be like in another ten years! She'll be even stronger than me. Maybe even as strong as that Hannah girl."

Cathillian nodded. "It's amazing what you can do with good people around you. Speaking of which..." His hand motioned out toward the crowd of people gathered in the cave, planning a war.

"Well, I guess the update has good things and bad things. Let's have it," she said.

"Bast and Cleo are outside right now with Dante and Snow. They are watching out for any movement. Last night, Corrine and Brann healed you. After a few hours, I healed you. This morning, the kids healed you again, and I'm about to do another round. You're going to need all the energy you can get."

"What about all of you?" she asked. "You're gonna need your strength, too."

He smiled. "Bast and Cleo slept. Sam slept. Don't worry about all of us. We feel just fine. You, however, went on a deadly solo mission, and nearly got yourself killed. So how do you feel?"

"Better than ever, actually. Very well rested, thank you. I'm definitely ready to get up and get this over with. These people need peace." Cathillian helped her to her feet.

"Me too. I'd have to say they are well on their way," he said.

Arryn nodded. "I have no doubt about that. We have to be ready. Because they will come fully armed, and I'm the only one here who knows how to create a magical shield."

"Don't worry," he said, placing his hands on her shoulders and lightly rubbing them. "We can't fail, not with the team we have."

CHAPTER TWENTY-FOUR

Arryn, Cathillian, and Corrine all stayed hidden in the trees on the ledge of the mountain, and the tigers were far away, high in another tree. Bast and Cleo stayed on the ground, their eyes closed as they felt the vibrations in the earth for any changes.

The sun was at its peak when Arryn saw Bast look pointedly up at her, her eyes glowing blue.

Do we have incoming? Arryn sent.

Roughly two hundred. They are so close to one another that it's hard to tell, Bast replied.

Arryn shifted in the tree to get a better look. Off in the distance, she saw exactly what Bast had felt through the vibrations in the ground. An army approached, and behind that army were two figures on horseback. She was almost certain who one of the two were, but the other was a mystery.

Send word to Lorelei and Mariana that we have company, Arryn sent. Bast quickly climbed on a nearby horse and rode for the Daoine waiting in the sea.

As usual, Corrine was left in the trees as Arryn and Cathillian went to the ground. They ran to the edge of the mountain and jumped down onto a small ledge that she, Bast, and Cleo had created. There was a path of them leading all the way down the wall, allowing them a safe journey to the ground without using more magic than necessary.

When Arryn finally hit sand, she ran toward the front line with Cleo.

"Lorelei and Mariana are in the water, ready to go. Bast should be back in no time," Cleo said.

Before Cleo had even finished her sentence, Bast was returning on horseback, jumping off and slapping the horse's rear to send her running somewhere safe.

"Lorelei and her group are ready. If we get overwhelmed, we throw them toward the ocean. Her group will take them down. Mariana will call a storm if needed, but she is anticipating Selena running away. If that happens, she said she has to cut and run," Bast reported.

Arryn nodded. "I wouldn't expect anything less. She is here for Selena and her crew. We will do our best to keep them here, but if Selena tears ass out of here, Mariana has every right to go."

Cleo nodded, her entire body vibrating in anticipation.

"Are you okay?" Arryn asked.

"I'm not sure if I'm excited or scared to death," Cleo said.

Arryn smiled. "Both. And that's fine. You've never taken on an opponent this large before. In the Dark Forest, it was much different; we had an army of druids on our side. Speaking of people on our side, has anyone seen Samuel?"

Bast and Cleo looked at one another, obviously clueless. Arryn turned to Cathillian, who only shrugged his shoulders.

"Seriously? No one knows where Samuel is?" Arryn asked with worry creasing her brows.

"He said he had something to do, and I haven't seen him since," Cathillian said. "He's a big boy, so I figured he could handle it, whatever it was."

Arryn sighed heavily. "Except we are heading into *war*. They could have caught his short, grumpy little ass and strung him from a tree by now."

"Uh, I'm worried about the little shit, too, but our guests have arrived, and they are heavily armed. Maybe we should focus on the here and now," Cleo said.

Arryn turned to see that the enemy had quickly descended upon them. Only a quarter-mile remained between the two forces. She could sense the energy radiating from the amphorald crystals.

She nodded. "Cleo is right. We don't have time. We'll have to find him after."

"Tell me again how we plan to stop a wall of magitech weapons?" Bast said.

Arryn smiled as her eyes flashed white. *Now*, she sent telepathically to the trees. "Oh, we have that covered. Someone was a little too persistent in wanting to help."

As Arryn finished speaking, half a dozen vines shot out of the trees on the ledge of the mountain. They spiraled down, grabbing weapons and yanking them back into trees before new vines repeated the process.

"Is that Corrine?" Cleo asked.

Arryn nodded. "Yep. And if they get too close to the water, Brann can do the same with seaweed—though not as strongly."

With a nod, Cleo said, "Then I guess that's our cue. Bast, let's go give the kids some backup."

The twins' eyes flashed blue as they jumped high in the air, one heading toward the base of the mountain, the other toward the edge of the ocean.

"Are you ready?" Arryn asked Cathillian.

"Are you kidding? Of course I am."

Arryn could feel the apprehension rolling off him, but she decided not to call him on it. Mostly because she felt it, too.

"Good. Then let's go," she said.

Snow and Dante arrived, and Arryn and Cathillian each

climbed on one's back. Both of the big cats lurched forward, their riders equipped with bows. Cathillian's had been crafted just that morning.

As they rushed forward, Arryn saw the twins moving in tandem as the oncoming guards ran in either direction toward them. A wave of sand lifted from the beach and was thrust toward the enemy. Just as in the previous instance the twins had done so, the men and women began to cry out.

Arryn and Cathillian took their bows from their shoulders, nocked arrows, and fired into the distracted crowd as Corrine continued to snatch weapons out of their hands.

Snow and Dante ran in a zigzag pattern, crossing one another's paths. Arryn and Cathillian continued to fire arrows, slowly picking off the enemy one at a time, as the twins continued to distract them.

Soon the Daoine rushed forward from the sea, their eyes glowing aquamarine as their hands began to move. Around the edges of the crowd closest to the ocean, the Daoine used their magic to surround the guards' and Raiders' heads in water.

The men and women flailed, struggling and unable to see as they drowned on dry land. As others in the crowd began to catch on to what was happening, they turned toward the Daoine, but the ocean dwellers were quick to retreat into the water to protect themselves.

Two shadows emerged overhead as Arryn and Cathillian continued to shoot arrows into the crowd. It wasn't a volley of arrows, but it was still effective while the enemy scurried about, trying to regain their vision. Most importantly, their method of attack *didn't require magic.*

The twins landed only a few feet away from Arryn, and Snow skidded to a halt. "How are you feeling? You didn't use too much magic, did you?" Arryn asked.

Cleo smiled. "Sand is much lighter and easier to work with

than earth. *We* feel great, but they sure as shit don't. They're pissed off and stumbling this way. We only have a few minutes."

"Did somebody say 'it'd be great ta have a rearick'?"

Arryn turned to see Samuel running up, battle axe in hand. "Nope. No one said that, but it sure as hell is. Where were you?"

"Yeah, Arryn thought your short, grumpy little ass was strung up in a tree somewhere," Cathillian said.

Arryn slapped him in the chest. "I said he *might* be. Anyway, we don't have time to fight amongst ourselves. We kinda have other engagements, in case you've forgotten."

Battle cries erupted out from behind Arryn—back from the way they had come. Confused, she turned to see nearly a hundred rearick rushing forward with excitement, their beards blowing in the breeze.

"Sam, I'm sorry I doubted you," she said.

He chuckled and nodded. "Ye sure as hell should be. These bastards were anxious ta get a taste o' revenge fer what those arseholes on the beach tried ta do in the Heights. They were happy ta come along. Ol' Tavich was right happy ta participate. We even took a shortcut. Glad we did."

Arryn nodded. "I'm glad you did, too; this wouldn't have been nearly as fun without you."

After clapping him on the back, Arryn turned to run toward the crowd, but was stopped by five explosions of magic.

Five men emerged from each one, teleported from somewhere unaffected by the sandstorm.

CHAPTER TWENTY-FIVE

Arryn's eyes flashed black, and she quickly deflected the first round of fireballs. The army of rearick quickly descended upon the new attackers. Another round of fireballs went out, and several rearick got hit as she, Cathillian, Samuel, and the twins rushed forward.

They made their way around the guards. The battlefield was more congested than Arryn had ever experienced, and she was forced to take advantage of whatever position she could find.

As she neared one of the guards who had been distracted by the wall of smaller, stout warriors, she pulled a ram's horn blade from the sheath on her hip and thrust it into the man's side. He quickly rounded on her as she pulled her knife free, and Samuel struck him from behind.

"Thanks, Sam!" she said.

"Don't mention it. Ye might wanna get the one behind ye, though," he replied as he pointed behind her.

Arryn turned and narrowly missed a sword thrust. She quickly dodged to the side, her movements clumsy as she kicked at his arm to keep the sword from hitting Samuel. She then ducked down, punched him in the stomach, grabbed his arm, and flung him over her back. A moment after she disarmed him, the crowd of rearick trampled him.

Within seconds, the group of attacking magicians were dead on the ground, and Arryn had found her way to the front line. She stalked forward, leading the army behind her as their enemies ran toward them.

Stay back, she sent to Corrine.

Arryn felt Corrine's annoyance through the mental link they shared, but she did as Arryn had asked.

Picking up her pace, Arryn charged for the first men in line. Knives in hand, she ducked down at the last second, plunging one into a guard's right side before sinking the other into his chest.

As he fell to the ground, three more turned on her. She thrust her foot hard into the knee of the first one before throwing an elbow into the face of the one coming up behind her. As the third approached, she dodged his swinging knife and planted her foot directly on his chest. The man stumbled back, and she quickly threw her knife.

Her bad posture and impatience caused the handle of the knife to hit her target, rather than the blade.

Her eyes widened. "Well, that's new."

"And a big fucking mistake," came a threatening voice to her left—the man whose knee she had attempted to take out.

"Yeah, not in the mood to die today. But thanks," she replied quickly.

Leaping into the air, she planted her left foot into his chest and pushed off, throwing her into the man whose nose she had broken. Caught off guard, the man fell to the ground, and she quickly punched him in the throat. The way he coughed, she knew she had successfully crushed the larynx. He wouldn't be a problem anymore.

Before she was able to celebrate, strong hands gripped both of her arms and pulled her to a standing position, holding her back flat against a man's chest.

The guard she had tried to kill with the terrible knife throw stood in front of her—ram's horn blade in-hand.

Her eyes faintly began to cloud over as she allowed the briefest of his thoughts to wash over her. With all the carnage and mayhem happening around them, he didn't seem to notice. When she had what she wanted, she decided to push him. He was irrational, and that would be his downfall.

She smiled. "Ah! Ya found it. Thanks so much. I tried to stab some ugly asshole, and I must've dropped it. Clumsy me!" His eyes narrowed as he growled in response to her comment. Feigned shock crossed her face. "Oh, Bitch. I'm so sorry. Was that you?"

"Stop stalling and do it already!" the man holding her shouted.

She smiled again, seeing the flash of his thoughts again. "Yeah. What he said."

The man let out a loud battle cry as he lifted the knife, ready to plunge it into her chest. As his arms arced over his head—giving her the clean shot she needed—her eyes flashed black, and her hand balled into a fist.

She jerked her hand, and the knife was yanked from his grip, sinking deep into his neck. She stomped down hard on the foot of the man holding her and whipped her head back, breaking his nose.

She reached forward and grabbed the knife from the neck of her other opponent as he fell to the ground. As she turned to face the man who held her captive, he punched her hard across the face. She felt the bone in her cheek break, and her vision immediately blurred in that eye.

That was about all she could handle.

As he grabbed her by her long braid, wrapping it around his hand and yanking her backwards, he was met with coal black eyes. His own eyes widened just a half second before she smashed a bright blue fireball into the side of his face.

He immediately let go, stumbling back and screaming loudly.

She ran forward and quickly ended his life. Then she took a deep breath and assessed her surroundings.

She caught sight of several bodies flying through the air toward the ocean, and the crowd parted enough for Arryn to see Bast and Cleo, their blue eyes blazing, as they kicked several asses at once.

Rearick all over were battling with guards and Raiders, battle axes sinking deep into the chests of their enemies. Samuel was among them, and she couldn't help her awe as she watched all of them fight together.

Cathillian was fighting three on his own, and she was about to run over to help, when he skewered two at once, pulled his blade free, then spun and sliced the head off the other.

And to think... I was about to come save you, she sent to him.

His eyes only briefly met hers, a subtle smile on his face as he responded. *You're good, but don't forget who trained you all these years.* He winked before rushing toward another foe, sword raised.

She rolled her eyes and smiled as she turned and ran farther in.

Only staying connected to a single person at a time was keeping the headaches at bay. She didn't even feel the faintest tingling of pain.

I wonder if that means I'm making progress.

The crowd of guards suddenly parted as several explosions of magic erupted. At least ten men teleported into the middle, holding strange devices in their hands.

She squinted her eyes as she came to a stop, struggling to see past the glowing blue amphoralds within them to identify the casing. Then she saw thumbs moving toward a button, and her eyes widened.

Her eyes flashed black as she turned and shoved out an incredible blast of power, throwing the first several lines of people back into the next as she created a barrier behind her.

But it had been a trap.

The men behind her teleported again, splitting in half and reappearing on either side of her as they threw the grenades into the crowd. They didn't care that their own men were caught in the fray; they only wanted blood.

It was the fight in the forest all over again.

Arryn's fear for the ones she loved got the best of her. *"COR-RINE!"* she screamed, both out loud and through the link, urgency taking her voice to a higher pitch than even she had been aware she possessed.

As the first blast erupted, vines shot out of the trees and wrapped around Cathillian, Samuel, and the twins. Vines came for her, too, but she deflected them. It was bad enough that she couldn't guarantee the safety of more than her closest friends; she wasn't about to abandon the fight out of fear for her own life.

Arryn arced both arms over her chest as the men vanished once again. A barrier enclosed around her as her hands shot out.

At the sound of another explosion, she forced herself to ignore the fire, smoke, and body parts raining down as she used her energy to search for the amphorald crystals.

People were scurrying all over, screaming as they struggled to climb over the next person to get away. It was total chaos. She realized just how lucky they all were that the grenades hadn't been made by Waylon or Elon.

Had they been, the explosions would have happened almost immediately, and everyone would be dead. These were poorly made by half-assed engineers, which gave them a slower response time. They were more than likely on a timer.

There!

She found the crystals. With a flick of her hands, the grenades lifted from the ground, the crystals glowing an almost blinding blue.

Elon had taught her a great deal about engineering such weapons; though she could never build one herself, she knew each part had a job to do. Without even looking into them closely, she knew that with every tick of the timer, something tightened down on the crystals inside. The timers were all set differently, and poorly crafted, but they were about to reach the crystals' breaking point, which would cause them to explode.

Looking back over her shoulder, she found a large concentration of guards that hadn't yet joined the fray. As soon as they saw her face, they began to run back toward their camp.

Twisting around, Arryn launched the grenades forward with her magic. She clenched her fists as they landed, and the telekinetic energy tightened around the grenades—the tiniest bit of pressure being all they needed.

Reinforcing her shield, she closed her eyes and turned her face away as the explosions began. Seven grenades detonated, raining ash, sand, blood, and various body parts all around.

She held herself together by reminding herself that it was exactly what those bastards had planned to do to the people she needed to protect.

Her eyes flashed white as she searched the trees. *Is everyone okay?* she asked Corrine.

Safe and sound, the young druid responded.

Good. Get Cathillian and the others down here. We have a fight to finish.

CHAPTER TWENTY-SIX

L orelei watched in horror as explosions erupted. There were two at first, detonated inside a cluster of fighters from both sides.

The enemy had blown up their own men.

The darkness that humans were capable of never ceased to amaze her. Watching Arryn and her group work, however, reminded her that not all outsiders were bad.

There were several moments when she and the Daoine villagers were stuck just waiting. During those times, she watched in awe as Arryn used incredible magic to overcome the evil men coming to kill them.

The forest druid wasn't the only one.

Though Lorelei didn't like it, Brann was in the water, waiting for those who might wander too close. He would use his magic to wrap seaweed around their ankles and drag them into the ocean, where another Daoine villager would take over the fight.

Lorelei didn't like the idea of him fighting at his age, but she knew he had been forced to kill men before, to save the life of his sister. This wasn't new to him, but it also wasn't something he needed to see.

Still, he had demanded to be a part, and she knew without a doubt that he would find a way to do so with or without her permission, which would have only put him in danger. At least with him next to her, she could watch him, protect him, and send him away if she needed to.

Several more explosions rocked the beach, and Lorelei turned to see dozens of men dying as they scurried away, running back in the direction from which they'd come.

Part of her was disgusted, but she would never forget young, innocent Katie, killed for the sake of a message, or her mother, dying to alleviate her grief. Lorelei would never forget the devastation on Arryn's face as she eased the woman from this life into the next.

While the Elder knew it had killed a part of Arryn to do it, she was grateful to her for easing her cousin's suffering.

As men continued to scatter, trying to get out of the way of any other impending explosions, they began to stray too close.

"*Now!*" Lorelei shouted.

She and the other villagers in the water thrust their hands forward, pulling water from the air and drowning their enemies on dry land. Brann went to work pulling some of them in, and other villagers grabbed hold and took his targets further out to sea.

Thunder cracked somewhere in the distance, and Lorelei turned. Brann's eyes were already wide as he turned in the direction the sound had come from.

"They're fleeing!" he shouted, as he pointed to a few small boats heading toward the Raider ship.

Out of her peripheral, Lorelei saw movement on the beach, just at the edge of the water. She turned to see Mariana and several of her crewmates running over.

"I'm sorry, I'm going have to pull my men and go," Mariana said disappointedly. "I truly hoped this wouldn't happen, but I can't let them get away again."

Lorelei nodded. "Do what you have to. Your men have already helped more than you realize. Thank you."

Mariana nodded, her eyes glazing over sea green. "I'm not finished yet."

The Storm Caller stepped into the sea and placed the end of her staff in the sand. Her eyes flashed even brighter as thunder cracked directly overhead. Clouds quickly appeared, as lightning webbed across the sky.

Lorelei watched as Mariana tightened her hands on the staff, burying it further into the sand. At the same time, lightning reached down from the sky, striking two men. Then a third... and then three more.

The Storm Caller repeated this a few times, causing the enemy to scatter. The Daoine villagers quickly swam up the coast. In a flash, they were able to meet the fleeing guards and pull them into the sea.

"That's incredible," Lorelei said in wonder.

Mariana's eyes faded back to their natural color as she smiled down at the Daoine woman. "Thank you. And now we have to go."

"You should take Arryn," Brann piped up. "You'll be able to do twice as much damage with her on board; you've seen what she can do. If you want to catch up to the ship and take it down, you'll need her."

Mariana looked toward the other ship. She couldn't see well, but from what she could make out, they were still boarding.

Finally, she nodded. "I think you're right. It's time to end this for good. I never want to see that ship again."

"Let's do this," Arryn said, running up. "I'll sink that bitch to the bottom of the sea."

Brann waved to her excitedly, and she looked over at him and winked.

"You got here quick. Do you still have enough magic?" he asked.

She smiled. "Well, I couldn't ignore your mental screaming. For some reason, your thoughts cut straight through my head—that sounds like a complaint, but I'm quite happy about it. It saved a lot of trouble. And believe it or not, I haven't really used much magic. The barrier was most of it. I think I still have enough juice to sink a ship."

Mariana nodded. "Glad to hear."

Arryn held up a finger. "But before we go… Brann, I think I have a job for you. For *all* of you."

CORRINE WAS ESCORTED BACK into the cave, though not before she healed Arryn. The Arcadian druid hadn't used much magic, but that was only because she hadn't been healing her wounds either. She had sustained several bruises, cuts, and her right cheek bone had been broken.

The healing helped rejuvenate her energy as well as improve her sight. Despite Arryn's continuous worry for Corrine, she knew the girl worried about her just as much.

The battle on land had completely wrapped up once Selena and Esmerelda began making their escape. It was obvious that the women had no plans to take anyone else with them, though she was certain they wouldn't turn down help if they managed to catch up to the ship in time.

Arryn couldn't imagine serving someone so cold and cruel. They were no better than Alaric and his brother, or Talia, or Adrien. Each of them had been more than willing to sacrifice their own people if it meant they came out ahead. It disgusted her.

She was glad this Storm Caller seemed to be different. Mariana and Captain Veren were readying everyone onboard for what was about to come.

"Do you really think they can pull it off?" Mariana asked her as she approached.

Arryn looked over the edge of the ship and saw several Daoine swimming down below. Others were farther out in the water.

She nodded. "I do. Let's get the ship going. We aren't going to find out anchored here."

Cathillian walked up, his eyes flashing green as Mariana's turned blue green. Once again, storm clouds began to rise as they combined their magic. The wind blew against the sails, as Mariana held tighter to the staff she had placed in the cup of water.

The ship began to turn and make its way farther out to sea. Arryn could see Selena's storm from miles away, but the enemy Caller didn't have what Mariana had. She didn't have Cathillian.

Mariana's ship raced across the water, and Arryn was awestruck. She had never been on a boat, let alone a large ship. It was fascinating to her. The scent of the saltwater mixed with the storm overhead, and it was beyond exciting. Somehow, Cathillian's storm smelled like the forest when it began to rain, and it felt like home. The forest meeting the ocean.

Looking over, Arryn couldn't tell if beads of sweat had formed on Mariana's face, or if it was ocean water. Strict concentration furrowed the Storm Caller's brows and flared her nostrils.

"We're getting close," Arryn said. "Don't exhaust yourself, but stay focused."

Mariana and Cathillian both nodded, Cathillian's eyes flashing even brighter.

Arryn looked over the edge of the ship, and her eyes widened. An entire pod of dolphins was swimming just below the surface of the water, leaping out, and then diving back in. It was beautiful, but she knew why they were there.

She too could sense Brann close by.

He had gone out with his family on her orders. They were to keep close until she said otherwise. If things went the way she planned, she would need their help to get free of the water.

"Get ready, Arryn," Bast said. "Are you sure you don't want us to go with you?"

She turned back and nodded. "Trust me, you don't want to be on that ship when I bring it down."

Bast hesitated for a moment, then nodded and stepped back.

Facing forward again, Arryn watched as the storms collided. The coast was long gone, and all that existed now was the wide-open sea. Anxiety began to prickle in her belly, and she took several deep breaths to calm herself.

Her eyes flashed green as she added even more wind to the sails. She wondered how it was possible that they hadn't torn, or the masts hadn't broken, but that was a worry for another time.

Selena's ship was now close enough that Arryn could see the few men and women who had managed to escape, scurrying about on board. They were preparing for battle, but they had no idea what they were in for.

Black faded into the green of Arryn's eyes, and her magic exploded around her, transporting her from the bow of Mariana's ship to the stern of Selena's. Six men ran for Arryn, but her arms thrust forward and moved to the left in a sweeping motion. Wind slammed hard into their sides, throwing them overboard.

Arryn didn't need to know what happened after that. The Daoine were sticking close, just as she had asked.

Several knives were thrown in her direction by those who were too afraid to approach directly. With a telekinetic shove, the knives were thrown back at their owners. Most did not penetrate, but a few men dropped to the ground from their wounds.

Begin, Arryn sent to Lorelei. *Swim hard and fast.*

Breaking her link with the Daoine, Arryn quickly linked to Mariana. *Back off. You don't want to get caught in this.*

Mariana began to protest, but Arryn broke the link, focusing hard on the task before her. She stepped forward, walking down several steps as guards and Raiders alike backed up, fear on their faces as they raised their weapons.

"A party? For me?" Arryn said with a smile.

Esmerelda appeared on the bow, enraged with her forces. "What are you doing? It's one girl! *Kill her!*"

The men and women looked at one another for a moment as they debated what to do.

Then, Arryn felt it. The first lurch in the ship.

She smiled as she arced both of her hands over her chest, then pulled them away as two fireballs surrounded them. She looked up and threw them both, striking at the sails. The fire raged, quickly devouring the fabric despite how wet it had become.

She heard an angry, "*No!*" shouted from the front of the ship and was happy to see Selena losing her mind. The Storm Raider's magic would no longer serve her. With no sails, she was stuck, forced to surrender to the Daoine people below.

The ship lurched again, and then began to turn. The ship was slowly rising on the edge of a whirlpool, turning slightly on its side as it did. Arryn could see the rushing water off the side of the ship, and the twisting clouds above.

Arryn smiled. "Enjoy the ride."

Her eyes flashed again as she turned toward the twisting water below. Her arms moved fluidly as she once again swept them to the right. Ribbons of water lifted from the surface of the sea, turning into bendable ice.

Arryn took a deep breath as she flicked her right wrist, darting ropes of ice forward and wrapping them around the group of men coming for her. The ropes hardened, and she anchored them to the ship.

As the remaining crew began to realize there was no escape, they began to claw and fight one another to get below deck. Surprisingly, Esmerelda and Selena stayed put, staring daggers at her.

"What's the matter?" Arryn asked as she walked forward, carefully measuring every step as the ship began to lurch again. Every time she planted her foot, she twisted her fingers to bring the ice over her boot and freeze it to the deck until she took her next step.

She had to focus on the women in front of her to keep from getting sick as she watched the spinning surroundings. Mariana's ship came and went, and then again, as Selena's ship rode nearly sideways into what was quickly becoming a massive maelstrom. It wouldn't be long before Arryn would be able to take the ship down completely.

"This is where it ends?" Esmerelda asked.

Arryn nodded. "You had an opportunity when your husband was killed; you could've used your terrible experiences to become an advocate for the downtrodden. Instead, you chose to be just like him."

Esmerelda only smiled, shaking her head as she met Arryn's statement with silence.

"You might be fine with dying, but I'm not," Selena spat to her leader.

The Storm Raider's eyes flashed, and lightning webbed across the sky. Arryn surrounded herself with a shield just before a wave of water crashed over the side of the ship.

A barrier wouldn't save her if a bolt hit the deck—charging the water beneath her feet.

Arryn leapt as high she could, unsure if this would work or if she was about to kill herself. Lightning crashed to the deck as her eyes flashed black. Just before she landed, ice ropes wrapped around her ankles to anchor her to the ship as a torrent of air twisted around her body. Staying afloat was already draining her, so she had to move fast.

Get ready! she sent to Lorelei.

Arryn grunted as she flung her arm forward, and frozen shards of ice whipped out of the maelstrom, impaling Esmerelda and Selena as she anchored them to the ship as well. Finally, Arryn screamed as she sent a blast of telekinetic energy straight down into the deck of the ship, blowing it apart.

Water began to rush in, and within seconds, the ship turned over, and Arryn was thrown into the maelstrom. Something struck her in the head, knocking her unconscious, as she was pulled deeper down and thrown about like the debris from the ship as the ocean swallowed them whole.

EPILOGUE

When she finally awoke, Arryn found herself lying on the beach with the sun shining down on her. She vaguely recalled being grabbed by several people and carried through twisting currents back toward the other ship. Slowly, her eyes opened, then she sat bolt upright to be met by faces all around her.

Mariana, Veren, and their crew were sitting off to the side, and her own group was hovering closely around her.

"I know I shouldn't be surprised, but I am," Samuel said.

"I wish I could've been there!" Corrine said enthusiastically. "They told me all about it, and I'm so mad I wasn't there!"

Arryn shook her head, fighting a migraine. "That was not a place you wanted to be, believe me."

"Thank you," Mariana said. "I have been hunting that ship for months, but every time we got close, they would flee."

"And because of you, we can feel safe again," Lorelei said. "Thank you for everything you did to help us."

"We were all just in the right place at the right time," Arryn shrugged groggily as she closed her eyes from the brightness of the sun. "We saved potentially hundreds of lives from their influence. We all deserve credit."

Cathillian hissed a little. "Yeah, but not all of us crushed a ship while flying."

Arryn laughed. "Slacker."

"So, what's next?" Lorelei asked.

"Yeah, where will you guys go now?" Brann asked.

Arryn yawned. "First, we nap. I need sleep. Then we go to Kemet and fight whatever is going on there. Speaking of, we are going to need to find a way southeast," Arryn said.

"I might know a ship willing to take a few kind souls in that direction," Mariana smiled.

Arryn nodded as she sighed. She collapsed back into the sand, putting her hands under her head as she closed her eyes. "That sounds great. Thanks. Oh, and don't let me forget to test this damn bracelet. If I don't send a message to Margit, bad things will happen."

"Maybe you can try to send Amelia a message, as well," Cathillian said. "She could pass one on to the Dark Forest, instead of us having to send Echo."

Cathillian had barely gotten his last words out, when Arryn quietly moaned *'mmhmm'*. Then she drifted back to sleep under the peaceful warmth of the sun, surrounded by her friends.

FINIS

WOW!!! It's been a LONG time, guys! It's kind of hard to believe how long it's been since I published an AoM book. Sorry about that! So, an update… lots of things have happened since I wrote one of these.

First: December 29, 2017, we signed on the house I grew up in! Long story, but this is actually the third time I've lived there. It was owned by someone else the last time, and I was renting it when it went through a foreclosure. We moved into a duplex for a year, and my house went up for sale just in time for our lease to run out.

Here's the cool part… Because of you guys—because of the KGU—I was able to buy back my home. My childhood home. Every day I wake up there, I go out to my office and work. I get to look out my back window and see the MASSIVE tree that I planted with my mom when I was a little girl. So, I deeply appreciate the support. When I say that… I absolutely mean it. You guys and LMBPN have been nothing but a blessing.

Next. I've been busy… I have been writing like crazy. It's April 10th, and I have Into the Maelstrom publishing tomorrow and the second (third counting the prequel) book in my Therian Chronicles series publishes FRIDAY! Two books in less than a week. Boom. My goal is the get two more books out this month (one in each series) but that's a lot to do in one month. We shall see, and I'll keep you updated!!

For those interested in checking out the series... They ARE available on KU (the prequel isn't YET, but it's only .99c). And you can find them here:

Origin (Prequel): books2read.com/u/mVZorP

The Dark Professor (book 1): books2read.com/u/mqpYDO

I'm very excited for that series! So many cool things happening in it already. Book three will be out April 27th! Not too much longer. I'm excited to see what it can do!

Now for the future of Arryn... I have ten books planned, potentially twelve, though I am planning to do a small series on Corrine as well. I have lots of plans. But now that Arryn is heading for Kemet, we will see a whole new world open up. I wish I could talk about it, but I can't!!! Michael Anderle helped me figure out exactly what I wanted to do. I had some ideas, but I wanted something REALLY cool and REALLY set apart from other series. And damn it... Michael delivered. I'm so fucking excited and I know all of you will love it. Because he's a genius haha!

Thanks to everyone again for sticking by my side and reading this series. And thank you to everyone that's been reading the new series!!! You're amazing!

Don't forget to check out The Candy Shop: Candy Crum Fan Club Facebook group for updates and fun stuff like sneak peeks on covers and things like that.

See you next time! <3

THANK YOU for reading all through the story, and through these author notes as well.

I am a big believer in supporting people working their asses off to accomplish good things in their live(s) and working to do better for their children. I am very aware that not all opportunities exist for all people. However, I'm also very aware not all people take the opportunities in front of them, or quite early.

Candy didn't give up when she wrote and published her books starting a LONG time ago. You remember a few of the stories in the Bible where someone was promised a blessing, and they 'just about' gave up before their blessing was delivered?

THAT is Candy's story in a nutshell.

She worked eight (8) years on her stories, trying time and time again to get a story out which readers would read and sell well enough to continue the series. The challenge (and there are a lot of challenges in our profession) beat against her for *EIGHT YEARS*.

She was not successful

Candy was to the point of giving up. (Hell, I probably would have after eight years – I suck like that.)

As Candy was contemplating throwing in the towel, she got the job of editing Chris (CM Raymond) and Lee's (LE Barbant) Rise of Magic series in order to bring in any extra income she could for her boys. From there, she was an integral part of their success and effort and was invited by those guys to write in the Age of Magic in the Kurtherian Gambit Universe...and if you are reading these books, you know the rest.

Candy brings her own version of WONDERFUL!!!! to our little happy family (I give her SUCH grief over her massive use of exclamation points. Now it seems like it has become a damned meme).

I still remember when she and I worked out the tweaks to her character and the series name, "The Feisty Druid" came about. I was driving back from Austin to Dallas when we had those conversations.

I believe it was just under a year ago or so that we were talking... In indie publishing, that feels like a decade.

I'm going to give Amazon major KUDOS for providing the Indie Writers the tools and infrastructure to create our own publishing businesses. Whether it is just one person publishing their book, or something a bit larger...all the way to our size at LMBPN Publishing.

If Amazon had not created the KDP system so many of us would not have the life we do today, and likely Candy would not have her family home back.

Amazon has facilitated the opportunity for creatives like Candy and myself to write stories and put them on sale through their distribution tools to get them in front of you, the fans.

But without you supporting us like you have? Well, I wouldn't be in this home I'm sleeping in tonight, either.

We wouldn't have had Bethany Anne or any of the other stories.

I always tip my hat to you, the fans. This time, I'm going to also tip my hat to Amazon for making what we do possible. As a reader, the first time I was able to just order 'book 02' of a series from my Kindle (DX) and start reading right away?

It was a magical experience.

I wish I had been smart enough to buy Amazon stock way back then, but I was too busy reading to be bothered with something like potential future wealth.

Or sleep.

Or even eating sometimes.

I'm blessed that Candy was afforded this opportunity to grow her own publishing company. I appreciate another feather in the Kurtherian Gambit Fans' hat of author lives you have changed.

Thank you from all of us.

Ad Aeternitatem,
Michael Anderle

CONNECT WITH THE AUTHORS

To see ALL of Candy's different books check out her website below

Website:
http://www.candycrumbooks.com

Facebook
https://www.facebook.com/groups/thecandyshopgroup/

Michael Anderle Social

Website:
http://www.lmbpn.com

Email List:
http://lmbpn.com/email/